With tantalizing slowness, he carried her to the brass bed. . . .

The soft rays of sunlight that filtered through the sheer material of the drapes reflected a glistening shimmer across her skin.

They came into each other's arms once more, and as his passion mounted, he embraced her boldly against his bare frame, a tender light shining through his eyes. His mouth moved down the length of her, sending hot shafts of desire racing unchecked through both of them.

Maybe nothing in the world could stop him from claiming her. Maybe these crazy feelings they were experiencing would turn out to be the real thing.

Maybe . . . she was finally in love.

Tale of Love

Lori Copeland

A DELL BOOK

Published by
Dell Publishing
a division of
The Bantam Doubleday Dell Publishing Group, Inc.
666 Fifth Avenue
New York, New York 10103

ISBN: 0-440-20173-X

Printed in the United States of America

Published simultaneously in Canada

December 1988

10 9 8 7 6 5 4 3

KRI

To Emily Reichert:
for her support, guidance, and enthusiasm.

Tale of Love

Chapter One

THE SNOW WAS COMING DOWN IN heavy sheets at O'Hare International Airport. Perched in the glassed-in birdcage that was known as the tower, weary flight controllers were going into the last hour of their shift.

It had been one hell of a night.

During the past few hours the controllers had efficiently handled close to four hundred incoming and outgoing flights. Now, the controllers were enjoying a welcome lull in the frenzied air traffic. Planes were sitting at the gates, others systematically coming down on landing strips; but the rush was nothing compared to what it had been earlier.

From his vantage point high atop the airport terminal, Garth Redmond looked out on the red beacon lights moving about the runway and wished his shift were over. The cold he'd come down with two days ago was making him feel headachy and irritable. He still had another hour left before he'd be free to go home, kick back, and relax.

Garth glanced at the ground-surveillance radar and suddenly sat up straighter. A quick reading on the bright display indicated that a Pan American Boeing 727, still ten miles out, was coming in faster than usual. Garth quickly flipped a switch on the panel before him. "Approach, this is Ground. Clipper 242 looks to be coming in pretty fast. Does he have a problem?"

"Ground, this is Approach. Yeah, he's picking up heavy ice. He's been cleared to approach."

Garth glanced at the airport-surface radar and frowned. If Tim Matthews, the Approach controller, had accurate information, they were in trouble. Garth's ground-surveillance screen indicated an unidentified radar target

2

taxiing toward the approach end of the active runway.

Garth hurriedly reached for the binoculars and scanned the snow-covered taxiway. He swore under his breath as he saw the lighted section of a Global Airways DC-9 disappearing toward Runway 36 in the heavy snow.

"Global, this is Ground . . ." The sharp crackling at the other end took Garth by surprise. "Global, this is Ground. Do you read me?" The question was met with an ominous silence. Flipping a second button, Garth said curtly, "Local, we've got a problem. I've got a Global Airways DC-9 taxiing on parallel taxiway, and I'm not talking to him."

"What's he doing out there?" Jack Lindley shot back.

"That's what I'm trying to find out. Better advise the Clipper."

"Roger." The Local controller flipped a button on his panel. "Clipper 242, be advised we have a no-radio Global DC-9 taxiing southbound on Runway 36 parallel taxiway. Be prepared for a go-around."

Even while the Local controller was advising the Pan American pilot, Garth realized that the huge Boeing 747 coming in from Anchorage was on the final mile to mile-and-a-half approach. He seriously doubted he could go around.

"Local, what's the Global doing there?" the pilot of the Clipper demanded.

"That's what we're trying to find out."

Garth listened to the tense exchange as he kept a close eye on the runway visual-radar indicator. Visibility was down to two thousand, four hundred feet. For the past four and a half hours, the pilots had been relying solely on instruments.

Garth concentrated on the monitors. The nerves between his shoulder blades squeezed together painfully as he hit a button again.

"Global DC-9, this is Ground. Exit runway *immediately!* A Boeing 747 shot final!"

While the media focused on midair collisions and near misses midair, the more frequent problem that faced a flight controller was the kind of situation Garth now found himself monitoring. Wiping a shaky hand across the back of his neck, he eased forward in his chair as the tower supervisor threw down the papers he had been reading and came over to stand behind Garth's chair.

"What's going on?"

"I've got an unauthorized DC-9 taxiing into reserved runway, and I'm not talking to him."

Tale of Love

Joel Anderson's seasoned eyes quickly sized up the developing situation. He frowned.

"The fool apparently thinks he's been cleared to taxi," Garth muttered. He tried to reach the DC-9 again. "Global DC-9, exit to taxiway *immediately!* Repeat. Exit to taxiway *immediately!*"

Joel leaned over Garth's shoulder and watched the screen as the two planes continued on their landing courses, both simultaneously approaching Runway 36.

"Tell Local to advise Clipper to go around," Joel warned as Garth automatically started pressing the necessary buttons.

"Local, this is Ground. Advise Clipper 242. Unauthorized DC-9 still on runway. Go around *immediately!* Repeat. Go around *immediately!*"

"Roger!" Local quickly activated another button. "Clipper 242, this is Local. Aircraft on runway. Go around. Repeat. Go around."

Garth could hear Local talking to the Clipper. Then he heard the pilot's grim refusal. "I'd love to oblige, Local, but this ain't no crop duster I'm flying!"

"Oh, hell!" Garth's voice echoed bleakly in the darkened room as he sagged back in his chair. The DC-9 was about to cross the path reserved for the incoming Clipper; and with radio contact to the DC-9 gone, it was out of the flight controller's hands and up to a Higher Power.

All Garth could hope for was that the timing of the two aircrafts would be split second and a collision would be avoided.

Joel hurriedly reached for the crash phone to alert the fire station and emergency crew to the pending crisis. Garth tried to raise the Global DC-9 again.

"Global, exit to taxiway immediately! Repeat. Exit to taxiway immediately!"

Eyes riveted to the screen, Garth and Joel watched in tense silence as the two blips on the radar screen rushed closer and closer together. The room had grown unnaturally quiet as the other flight controllers performed their duties in hushed tones.

"Well, start praying," Joel advised.

The wide-bodied Boeing 747 touched down on the landing strip and came streaking along the runway as the DC-9 began to ease its way across. The pilot of the DC-9 was still unaware of what was happening.

"Move, damn it!" Garth spoke tautly to the DC-9, then held his breath as the plane continued to roll laboriously across the path of the incoming 747.

"Get out of the way, buddy!" The strained voice of the Clipper pilot cracked over the wire as he, too, tried to will the DC-9 out of his pathway.

The dots closed in on each other as the Clipper roared down the landing strip at a speed of more than two hundred miles an hour. The blips came closer and closer.

Suddenly, they split apart, and the DC-9 eased off the runway as the 747 shot by him in a screech of flying mud and snow.

Garth threw down his pencil angrily as Joel let out a loud war whoop.

"Holy Shi . . . What was that?" the expletive slipped out as the pilot of the DC-9 finally came in over the wire. He was obviously shaken.

"Global, you're on unauthorized taxiway!" Garth snapped, then curtly explained what had just happened.

The pilot made his apologies, then requested to return to the terminal. "We've had a radio malfunction."

Garth granted the necessary clearance and abruptly severed contact with the pilot.

For a moment Garth fought to overcome an

unreasonable sense of frustration. He fumbled for his handkerchief as Joel laid his hands on his shoulders and gave them a supportive squeeze. "Good work!"

Emotionally and physically drained, Garth could not will himself to respond to Joel's encouragement. He mopped the moisture from his forehead. There was no longer any doubt about it: The pressure of the job was getting to him.

True, Garth had experienced closer calls, but his heartbeat had never raced as fast as it was now.

"Another close one!" Garth's voice echoed hollowly in the dimly lit room.

Joel thought Garth sounded unusually tired and emotionally drained—not at all like the self-confident, cocksure young kid Joel had hired nine years ago. There had been a time when Garth would have brushed off this sort of incident without another thought, considering it just a part of the business. Tonight, though, was different. Garth seemed brooding, uncertain, troubled . . .

Joel's eyes met Garth's sympathetically. Garth was one of the most competent young men he had ever had the pleasure of working with. He was alert, intelligent, a seasoned professional. But as his supervisor, Joel couldn't sit back and ignore the situation any longer.

All the symptoms of burnout were there. Anxiety, stress, and the pressures of the demanding position were obviously taking their toll on Garth.

Joel clapped a friendly hand on the younger man's shoulder. "Step into my office when you get a minute."

Garth's pulse jumped erratically. "Sure, Joel." His eyes remained fixed on the screen as he spoke, but he knew what was coming. Joel had noticed his odd behavior, and he wanted an explanation. But Garth didn't have one.

By the time he entered Joel Anderson's cluttered cubicle a half hour later, he'd decided that he was blowing the situation out of proportion. He was fine. Joel wasn't going to yell at him. He probably just wanted to shoot the breeze for a while.

Joel was on the phone when Garth arrived. He glanced up and motioned him to help himself to the coffee.

Garth shook his head. The last thing he needed was more caffeine in his system. He settled his large frame in the chair opposite the desk.

In a few moments Joel finished his conversation and replaced the receiver. "Sorry about the delay. Those idiots in the office drive me up a wall."

Garth smiled. "No problem."

Joel got up and walked to the hot plate. "I shouldn't drink another cup of this stuff. Wanda would have a fit if she knew how many I've had today . . . but what the hell." He poured the strong black coffee into his cup and added a couple of packets of sugar. "I'm going to die of something, so I figure I might as well go happy."

Garth acknowledged Joel's attempt at levity with a wan smile and waited patiently until he sat down again.

Joel was always worrying about what his wife would say about his bad habits but never enough to change them, Garth thought with halfhearted amusement. He just wished Joel would get on with whatever he had on his mind.

It seemed to Garth that Joel was doing a lot of fidgeting before he got to the point. "You're doing one hell of a job, Garth," he finally said, lighting a cigarette absentmindedly.

Garth glanced up, surprised by the unexpected praise. He was still half expecting to be chewed out for his performance during the past few weeks. Joel hadn't missed his edginess—Garth would bet on that. But compliments?

"Thanks. I appreciate it."

"But you're going on excused leave." The statement was firm and straight to the point.

Garth shook his head. "No . . . I can't. Not right now."

"Sure you can. You're on leave beginning tomorrow morning."

"Come on, Joel . . ." He was about to argue the point, when he saw the look of determination in his superior's eyes.

Garth realized he could sit there and argue all day, but in the end Joel would have the last word.

"No buts, Garth." His tone might have softened, but his resolution hadn't. "I've sat by and watched what's been going on for weeks now, and I think it's time we did something about it."

Garth didn't have the heart to disagree or to press Joel for details. They both knew Garth hadn't been himself lately. But, damn, his ego sure hated to accept the fact that he was stressed out.

"I'm sorry. I know I haven't been giving you my best lately," he admitted.

Joel leaned back in his chair and studied his coffee cup thoughtfully. "I've never felt that you didn't give me your best. You're one of the most valued men I have. I'm only trying to see that you stay that way. You're tired and stressed out. I want you to get a little R and R. Relax, have some fun. Forget about the job and its pressures."

"Are you worried because of what happened a few minutes ago?" Garth asked. "Because if you are, I can explain. I have this miserable cold—"

Joel interrupted gently. "No, this is a decision I've been avoiding for weeks."

"You think I'm no longer competent?" The mute appeal in Garth's eyes was hard for Joel to ignore.

"Of course not. I just think you need a little rest." He could see that Garth was wrestling with his pride. "It's nothing to be ashamed of. We all have our limits. A few weeks of lying in the sun, and you'll be back complaining you've used up all your vacation time," Joel promised.

"Well, I can't say I agree, but you're the boss." Garth conceded, though he hated to.

"Then you agree to the leave?"

"I don't think it's a good time. It'll leave you in a bind," Garth reminded him. "I think if I could just get over this cold—"

"You will. A couple of weeks will work wonders for you." He leaned forward in his chair and stubbed out his cigarette. "Damn things are going to kill me," he complained under his breath. "Wanda would have a fit if she knew how many I've smoked today."

Garth stood up, openly disturbed by the unexpected turn of events. He felt resentful and deprived; yet at the same time he felt a strange sense of relief. Two weeks without coping . . . without worrying . . . without sitting on the edge of his chair . . . Maybe that *was* all he needed.

"Well, I don't suppose it would do any good to argue with you."

"Nope. None at all. Soon as Randy gets here, consider yourself out of work for the next two weeks. Or longer, if you need it. You let me worry about your replacement. That's what I get paid for."

"Joel . . . I appreciate this. . . ." He reached over to shake his superior's hand, gratified for the other man's concern.

"Don't worry about it," Joel said absently.

"Oh, Lord, look at the time! I've got to call Wanda and tell her I'm going to be a few minutes late." He flashed Garth an apologetic grin. "The woman's terrified I've dropped dead if I don't get home by six on the dot."

Garth knew exactly where he would go to find the privacy he wanted: his grandparents' beachfront cottage in West Creek, North Carolina.

Silas and Grace Redmond would be in Florida for the winter, but Garth knew how to reach them.

It didn't matter that he wouldn't be able to lie around in the sun—in West Creek, it was, after all, the end of December. All he needed was a good book, a couple of packages of Oreo cookies, and complete solitude for the next two weeks.

Keep the sun and sand—give me the seclusion of that cozy three-room cottage, he thought as he drove home to pack a couple of bags.

The time off would enable him to get his priorities back in line and his head on straight again. The weather wouldn't be all that bad in West Creek, and at least he'd be able get away from all this miserable snow for a few days.

Garth wasted no time in securing a plane reservation, packing, and calling a taxi. He figured it would be better if he left Chicago before the storm turned into a full-scale blizzard. Because of the holiday rush, Garth considered himself extremely fortunate to get a seat on the next plane. Fortunately, he had connections with a cute blonde at the ticket counter.

The nine-thirty flight would take him to Raleigh, where he'd have a brief layover before he could get a commuter hop to West Creek.

He decided to wait to call his grandmother from the terminal to ask her permission to use the cottage. If he called at the last minute, Garth knew she wouldn't have time to make half a dozen entertainment plans on his behalf.

Grace and Silas were well-meaning, but they always felt that Garth had to be entertained. Just because they were vacationing in Florida didn't mean Grace would be deterred from getting on the phone and lining up some of their friends to entertain her grandson in their absence.

At the last minute Garth made a hurried call to Lisa Matthews, the woman he'd been dating for the past few months. Lisa was another pressure that had been nagging at him lately. She wanted to get serious; Garth, on the other hand, was perfectly content to let the relationship drift along, with no strings attached. The unexpected change in plans would give him some desperately needed breathing space.

Garth hurriedly made the call, explaining to Lisa that he was going away for a few days.

She was upset but made Garth promise to call her the minute he arrived at his grandparents' cottage.

"Why don't I fly down for the weekend?" she suggested.

"No, I think I need the time alone, Lisa." They'd been spending so much of their time arguing lately that Garth felt he needed a reprieve.

"Well . . . if that's how you feel." Garth could hear the petulance creeping into Lisa's voice, but he chose to ignore it.

"I'll call you later in the week." It was Garth's one concession.

"Make sure that you do."

Fierce winds blowing off icy Lake Michigan raced a bone-rattling chill down Garth's slightly feverish body as he left his apartment thirty minutes later, lugging the suitcases. He paused, sneezed, then blew his nose before going on.

A heavy blanket of snow made a dull, crunching noise beneath his boots as he trudged through the white powder to the waiting taxi. With six inches already on the frozen ground, the National Weather Service wasn't calling for an end to the storm until late tomorrow night.

Garth cautiously shuffled along what he assumed was the unshoveled sidewalk. Getting through the wet snow proved to be no easy task—but, then, nothing had been easy lately.

The sound of the cabbie impatiently leaning on the horn made Garth quicken his steps. Struggling to retain his balance as well as the luggage, he felt his temper flare when he thought of how he had waited for that cab driver for more than an hour, and now the man had the audacity to honk for *him* to hurry!

Garth reached the cab and tried to jiggle open the door, which had frozen shut fifteen minutes earlier. Hoping to free a hand and pry the stubborn latch loose, he set one suitcase down beside him, where it promptly sank out of sight in a growing snowdrift.

Expecting the door to require a hefty-sized tug, Garth obliged with a hearty jerk that sent the door flying open. He suddenly found himself lying flat on his back.

"Oh, Lord, give me a break!" Garth pleaded as he lay staring up at the cab's muddy underside. Glancing around to see if anyone other than the cabbie had seen the humiliating incident, he slowly rolled back onto his feet.

Convinced that the driver wasn't overly interested in his welfare, Garth grabbed the suitcases and pitched them into the backseat. He had to slam the door twice before it finally latched.

The plump cabbie wrestled a nasty stub of cigar butt between his lips and asked with a distinct Jersey accent, "What's ya pleasure, Mac?"

"O'Hare," Garth requested curtly. *And, believe me, nothing's my pleasure at the moment!* he thought irritably.

The cabbie shot a sympathetic glance in the rearview mirror. "Rough day, huh?" He rolled down the window and reached out to wipe the thick frost from the windshield with a large rag.

Garth viewed the action with growing dis-

may. No defrosters in this kind of weather?
"You can see where you're going, can't you?"

"Huh? Oh, sure. The darn defroster went on the fritz about an hour ago. No sweat, though. I can get ya to O'Hare with my eyes closed." He gunned the engine, and the cab fishtailed onto the busy street.

The transmission sputtered as the driver raked through the gears. Every time the gears caught, the back of the taxi spun out, forcing Garth to grab the back of the seat for support.

"Hold on! This baby runs like a dream once you get her hummin'," the cabby called back between speed shifts.

Garth rested his head wearily against the seat and shot another squirt of decongestant up to his clogged sinuses.

As the cab neared the airport the traffic became congested and slowed to a snail's pace. Garth was sneezing with appalling regularity now.

"Sounds like you got a lulu of a cold there."

"Yeah, I think it's getting worse." Garth blew his nose, then glanced at his watch. He was going to be cutting it close. He was tempted to tell the driver to step on it, but he wasn't suicidal yet.

19

A good mile and a half from O'Hare the traffic came to a complete halt. Garth kept glancing uneasily at his watch. Twenty minutes later not a single car had budged.

"Hey, listen! I have an eight-o'clock plane to catch," he reminded the driver.

"Just keep your shirt on! I'll get you there, bub."

Another ten minutes passed, and Garth realized that time was running out. The plane would leave in twenty minutes, and he was still a half-mile from the airport.

Heaving a resigned sigh, Garth reached into his pocket, withdrew a wad of bills, and hurriedly paid the driver.

"Hey! Where you goin'?"

"I'll have to make a run for it." Garth sneezed again and grabbed the two pieces of luggage.

The long, cold run to the airport was a nightmare. The drifts were piling up, and the temperature was in the low teens. The tip of Garth's nose was beet-red, and his cheeks looked like two blazing cherries by the time he reached the terminal. He ran inside, wheezing like an overworked locomotive.

It was still a long sprint to his boarding gate. Garth was convinced that it was only through an act of divine intervention that the jetway was still attached to the plane when he arrived.

Stepping inside the plane, Garth was greeted by a friendly flight attendant. "Good evening. Welcome aboard American Airlines."

Garth fumbled in his pocket for his soggy handkerchief and tried to return her smile without his frozen face cracking into a million pieces. "Good evening . . . Terrible weather . . ." he returned lamely.

"I hope you enjoy your flight, sir."

I hope so too, Garth thought grimly as he dragged his baggage down the aisle—there had been no time to check it. He wedged the suitcases tightly into the crowded compartment at the rear of the plane.

Moments later, he sank wearily into his assigned seat. The two-year-old sitting next to him promptly started screaming as his mother tried to fasten him into a seat belt.

Short of a plane crash, Garth knew the flight had to be more enjoyable than the past four hours had been.

Chapter Two

HILARY BROOKFIELD WIPED HER teary eyes and tossed another soaked tissue into her purse. It joined nine crumpled others.

She hated herself for being so weak—so out of control—so asinine! She wiped angrily at the icy particles forming on the window and stared out of the cab into the blinding snow. Hilary had always considered herself an "in-charge person," but today's events had proved her to be anything *but* in control.

The yellow cab slowly inched its way through the snow-covered streets of Denver. The worsening weather had rendered the rush-hour traffic more snarled and congested than usual.

"How much longer before we get to the air . . . airport?" she asked, trying to subdue her sobs. Her warm breath turned frosty in the arctic air.

"I'll have you there in another twenty minutes. Sorry about the heater. It was working fine an hour ago. Can't imagine what could've happened to it," the driver apologized.

Hilary sighed. She could explain the malfunction—she'd been in the backseat for the last forty-five minutes of that hour. Why *shouldn't* the heater fall apart? Everything else in her life had, she thought, succumbing to another onslaught of self-pity. She bawled into her wadded tissue for a few minutes, then blew her nose again.

The taxi driver peered expectantly into the rearview mirror. If there was one thing that made Max Stinson nervous, it was a squalling female. Not that Max was hard-hearted. He was considered a real softie, but the poor soul in the backseat hadn't turned off the tap since he'd picked her up.

"Um . . . miss? Are you all right back th—"

KAABOOMMM!

Hilary squealed, then ducked at the sound of the sudden explosion.

"Oh, boy! I think we've got ourselves a flat tire, miss." The driver fought the steering wheel and finally managed to ease the cab over to the side of the road.

After bringing the crippled taxi to a halt, the man turned to reassure his passenger. "Now, don't you worry. I'll get you to Stapleton on time."

Hilary sat up and blew into her tissue again, skeptical of his optimism. Why should she hope she'd make her plane on time? Nothing else had gone right today.

She'd lost a button off her new coat and the stud to her gold earring; there had been a fifteen-hundred-dollar discrepancy in the books at work; and she'd been dumped.

A mere flat tire shouldn't upset her. Hilary leaned over and bawled harder into the tear-sodden tissue.

Every snowplow in Denver had been working nonstop for the past twenty-four hours. Six-feet-high drifts made curbside parking impossible, but the cab driver had managed

Lori Copeland

to pull as far off the road as possible. There was an endless string of irritated motorists inching past the disabled vehicle. They leaned on their horns as if that would somehow even the score for their frayed tempers.

"I'll have the tire changed in a jiffy," the driver promised as he got out and slammed the door behind him.

Hilary worked to stem the flow of her streaming eyes. With yet another Kleenex having bitten the dust, she dumped it into her coat pocket and fished out a clean one.

While the driver changed the tire, she sat in the frosty silence of the cab, watching the snow drift past the car window. The hypnotic effect of the swirling flakes dredged up thoughts of the unpleasant emotional scene she'd experienced only a few hours earlier.

Lenny Ricetrum. Lenny Ricetrum the Rat, she corrected herself. The big dirty rat, she corrected herself again, as if calling Lenny names would help.

Hilary had dated Lenny steadily for the past few months. And she had grown to care very deeply for him—or at least she thought she had until this morning.

Wasn't that just like love? Hilary agonized against the cold pane of the window, indulg-

26

ing in her own private pity party. You think everything is wonderful, and the next thing you know . . . it all blows up in your face!

Oh, she'd seen it coming, though she hadn't wanted to believe it. Lenny had always had a roving eye. Maybe that's why she'd found him so attractive, so exciting, so much fun to be with, despite his being brash and rough around the edges.

Hilary readily admitted that Lenny was a novelty. She'd never dated anyone like him, and she'd found the experience exhilarating.

But Meredith Lowry had apparently found him equally attractive.

Meredith was always hanging around the construction site where Hilary and Lenny worked. Ralph, an electrician at O'Connor's, had noticed that the bold redhead was making an obvious play for Lenny's attention. He had called it to Hilary's attention once or twice.

"Hey, Hilary! Ya better keep an eye on that little redhead. Looks like she's mapping out your man!" Ralph had tried to sound as though he were teasing, but even then Hilary had detected the underlying tone of seriousness in his words.

Hilary had kept telling herself that Lenny's

case of roaming eyes was just a passing thing. Nothing to get herself in an uproar over. Besides, she'd always prided herself on not being a jealous or possessive person.

But deep down, Hilary knew the reason she hadn't confronted Lenny and demanded he put a stop to his womanizing; she thought she loved him. Consequently, the problem hadn't gone away.

This morning she'd barely seated herself at her desk when Lenny had come into her office and dropped the bombshell.

He hadn't minced words or tried to lighten the impact of his cruel announcement. Without batting an eye, he'd announced that their relationship was over. He'd left a stunned Hilary slumped over her IBM, wondering what had gone wrong.

"Hilary . . . I'm sorry." Michael O'Connor, the owner of the construction company, had tried to comfort her. "I was afraid this would happen."

Hilary cried on his broad shoulder, praying he wouldn't say "I told you so."

"Mr. O'Connor, Lenny didn't even say why . . ." Hilary dissolved into tears as Michael put a strong arm around her shoulders.

"Sh, sh, little girl." Michael gently tried to

soothe her tattered pride. "Men like Lenny don't usually explain anything they do. I say good riddance to bad rubbish, as far as that bum is concerned."

Hilary tried to still her sobbing. She was a grown woman acting like a child. But at that moment, she'd felt like a street urchin. One who had just been stepped on.

At Mr. O'Connor's suggestion, Hilary had taken the rest of the day off. Sitting alone in her apartment she had knocked a big dent in her supply of tissues. She spent two hours crying, pacing the floor, crying, drinking coffee, and crying.

Realizing the situation wasn't improving, Hilary decided that what she needed was time away from the whole ugly situation. If she went back to the office, she would be forced to see Lenny at least a couple of times a day. She just didn't feel up to that right now.

With grim determination, she phoned Michael O'Connor and asked for a week's vacation to try and collect her thoughts.

"You go right ahead. A little time away is just what you need to put this thing in perspective," Michael agreed. "And don't feel guilty. Construction work is never booming this time of year. Enjoy your week."

Hilary decided she shouldn't waste precious time trying to decide where to spend her unscheduled vacation.

A good friend, Marsha Terrill, had moved to West Creek, North Carolina, a year ago. Hilary and Marsha hadn't been able to visit each other since Marsha's move, although they'd kept in close touch. Hilary decided that now would be the perfect time to visit Marsha.

The airline booked her on a nine-thirty flight. Hilary spent the next thirty minutes trying to reach Marsha. Each time she'd gotten a busy signal.

Hilary tried again before she left for the airport, but the line was still busy. Assuring herself that the layover in Raleigh would give her a chance to phone Marsha from the terminal, Hilary wasn't concerned. Marsha loved surprises, and besides, Hilary wasn't sure if she could control her emotions long enough to explain the unexpected visit.

Hilary's thoughts were interrupted as the cab driver got back into the cab. His clothing was covered with a thick dusting of snow.

"All fixed," he announced.

"Do you think we can still make it to the airport on time?"

"You bet! Even if I have to make this taxi

sprout wings to get you there. I've never caused any passenger to miss a flight yet."

Yes, but you've never had me in your cab before, Hilary thought fatalistically.

Max was true to his word. He delivered Hilary to the airport ten minutes before her plane departed. What he neglected to mention was that *she'd* have to sprout wings to make it through the gates in time to catch her flight.

She raced feverishly through the crowded terminal, dodging through the throng of holiday travelers. As she breathlessly neared the boarding gate, a slow-moving elderly gentleman ahead of her dropped his boarding pass. He came to an abrupt halt.

Hilary had no choice but to do the same. She drew in her breath painfully as she felt her right ankle twist as she struggled to regain her balance. The ankle had been broken in a skiing accident three years earlier, and the renewed pain was breathtaking. Fighting the hot sting of the wrenched muscles, Hilary started trying to pick up the luggage she had dropped.

"You okay, little lady?" The elderly man turned around, unaware that he had been the cause of her newest crisis.

"Yes . . . thanks . . . I'll be fine." Hilary gritted her teeth in agony.

"Shouldn't be in such a big hurry. That's what's wrong with the world today. Everyone's in such an all-fired hurry," the man complained as he proceeded down the corridor.

"And happy holidays to you too," Hilary muttered.

She carefully tested part of her weight on the injured ankle. The searing throb was horrible. She realized that the only way she could make the flight was to swallow her misery and hobble on.

By grace alone, Hilary managed to make it to the jetway seconds before it was detached from the plane.

Sinking gratefully into her assigned seat, Hilary buckled her belt to prepare for takeoff. She fought back the hot swell of tears that threatened to overcome her again.

Hilary, you have to stop this, she warned herself. Other women had been dumped and had lived through it. She would too.

Hilary gently rubbed her swollen ankle and wondered if she would be able to get her shoe back on if she slipped it off during the flight. Deciding to take the chance, she kicked off the two-inch black heel and wearily leaned her head back on the headrest.

If she'd had even the slightest inkling of how this day was going to turn out, she would never have gotten out of bed that morning.

Chapter Three

AT PRECISELY TEN THIRTY-SEVEN, the Boeing 727 carrying Hilary Brookfield landed in Raleigh, North Carolina.

A light snow was falling, and because it was beginning to cover the ground, Hilary couldn't help but wonder if the two-hour scheduled layover would drag out endlessly. She quickly dismissed the disturbing thought. Surely fate had been cruel enough to her today, she reasoned.

By now her ankle had swollen to nearly

twice its normal size. She sighed as she thought about how she'd detained the man sitting beside her while she'd had to slowly force her shoe back on, groaning in agony.

Her ankle hung over the shoe like sagging elephant hide. If she'd thought the pain was bad before—well, it was worse now. Recalling the catastrophic course her life had recently taken, Hilary tried to summon up a hint of optimism as she hobbled painfully down the jetway.

At least I can still hobble, she told herself. *And I can still see where I'm going,* she added encouragingly. As a rule, her contacts would be bothering her by now, but they felt pretty good. Hilary limped on with grim determination.

Her improved spirits lasted until she entered the terminal. Her eyes widened when she saw the energetic preschooler who was throwing a temper tantrum. He bolted rebelliously from his mother and dashed headlong in her direction. Trying to sidestep the oncoming human missile, Hilary felt a body hurl against her. The sudden impact knocked her breathless for a moment.

Purse and makeup kit went flying at the same time that Hilary's right eye went blurry.

Her hand flew up to try and catch the contact that had been dislodged, but the automatic reflex came too late.

"Frederick Lee! You stop that this moment!" The child's mother marched over to take the little boy by the scruff of the neck. "Just you wait until your father hears about this! Say you're sorry to this nice lady for bumping into her!" The woman turned apologetically to Hilary, who by now had dropped frantically down on her knees and was crawling around the floor of the terminal, searching for the missing contact.

"It's all right . . . I'm sure Frederick didn't mean any harm . . ." Hilary was as blind as a bat without her contacts. She welcomed the assistance of several thoughtful travelers who offered to help with the search. In the end, however, the contact was lost forever.

"I'm really sorry about your contact," the harried mother assured Hilary again. She had a firm clasp on the child now. Fascinated, little Frederick was watching Hilary crawl around on the floor.

"Don't worry," Hilary assured the young mother. "I have an extra pair at home." The misfortune meant that she would be half-blind during her stay with Marsha. But only *half,* she consoled herself, still fighting to hold on to her earlier spurt of optimism.

"I saweee wadeee." Frederick had turned sullen in the face of adversity.

"It's quite all right." Hilary's smile was tolerant as one of the gentlemen helping to search for the missing contact took her arm and assisted her to her feet. A renewed surge of pain shot through her ankle, and she bit her lower lip to keep from moaning. Smiling, she thanked the gentleman.

The lady and child merged into the crowd as Hilary gathered her belongings and limped steadfastly toward Gate 78.

As Garth stepped off the plane, he noticed that the runway was crowded with emergency vehicles and personnel. There were two ambulances, two fire trucks, and various pieces of emergency equipment poised on the landing strip Garth's plane had just come in on.

Garth frowned as he noticed Hank Resin coming down the jetway with a hurried stride. Hank had been employed at O'Hare years ago. He'd since married and moved to

Raleigh. Garth recalled that Hank had been one of O'Hare's top mechanics.

"Hey, Garth, ol' man! Were *you* on this plane?" Hank's friendly grin was spread all over his face as he reached out to clasp Garth's hand.

"Yes. How are you, Hank?" Garth's frown deepened. "What's going on?"

"Are you serious? You don't know?"

"Know what?"

"There was a little mechanical trouble with the landing gears. The pilot managed to get them working in time . . . but only seconds before he had to touch down. The ol' wheels popped out of the belly like a roasted turkey!"

Garth grinned lamely, but Hank noticed that his face had turned two shades paler. "No kidding? We were coming in under emergency conditions?"

"Yeah. Flying's a real hair-raiser sometimes, ain't it?"

Garth felt his stomach grow queasy. He'd noticed that the pilot had circled the airport several times, but the idea that the plane was in trouble had never entered his mind. He felt himself go weak with relief at the close call. With his nerves already ragged, he'd have been peeling the paint from the plane's interior had he suspected he was in the middle of a "hair-raiser."

It didn't matter that it was snowing again. All that mattered was that his feet were back on solid ground. At least for now, Garth thought. In another couple of hours he would be airborne again. The flight to West Creek would surely be without incident, he hoped fervently.

As he emerged into the brightly lit terminal, Garth was mumbling under his breath a reassuring litany of statistics proving that the skies were safer now than ever before.

He had to deftly sidestep a woman who was down on her hands and knees in the middle of the floor. Garth swore under his breath and wondered where some of the weirdos he saw in airline terminals ever got the money for a plane ticket.

A few steps later he felt his shoe crunch down on what felt like a piece of glass. He paused momentarily and lifted the sole of his shoe up for inspection. He frowned as he discovered the remnants of a piece of hard candy. On closer inspection, he decided it was a contact lens.

Flicking the lens off his sole, he hurried in the direction of Gate 78.

Tale of Love

* * *

Hilary stopped at the first pay phone she found. She rummaged in her purse for change to make the call to Marsha. All she could come up with was six pennies, a nasty-looking nickel that had part of a breath mint stuck on it, and a Canadian coin she had picked up somewhere.

By the time she had limped to the nearest coffee shop for change, and limped back, all the phones were in use again. Hilary waited patiently while a frazzled housewife gave final instructions to her husband and children. Hilary was sure the woman's family must have been as happy to have seen her leave as Hilary herself was when the lady finally ran out of time and had to dash to catch her plane.

Hilary dropped the newly acquired coins in the slot and tapped the numbers. She breathed a sigh of relief when she heard the phone begin to ring.

"Hello! This is Marsha!" Marsha's familiar voice came over the line on the second ring.

"Hi, Marsh! This is—"

Marsha's voice continued. "I'm sorry I can't come to the phone right now. Get this—I'm lying on the warm beaches of sunny Jamaica! At the sound of the tone, please leave your name and number, and I'll return your call when I get home in two glorious weeks!" Following the recorded message, there was a beep.

Hilary clamped her eyes shut in disgust and clenched the receiver tightly in her hands. Jamaica! How could Marsha do this to her!

Hilary hooked the receiver back in place and broke out into a new round of desperate sobs. With her right hand she fumbled blindly through the muddle of wadded tissues overflowing her purse. A clean one was not to be found.

Garth was just about to call his grandparents' number, when he heard the young woman using the phone beside him suddenly burst into tears. He eyed Hilary apprehensively and continued punching out the numbers.

Hilary laid her head on her coat sleeve and cried harder, oblivious to the crowd she was drawing.

Garth watched her from the corner of his eye, noting her unproductive search for a tissue. He reached for his handkerchief and offered it to her.

"Thank you," Hilary accepted the handkerchief gratefully. She promptly wiped her eyes, and Garth resigned himself to the fact that the white linen would be soiled with black mascara. Then he turned his attention away as he heard his grandmother's voice come over the wire.

"Gram? Hi, it's Garth."

"Garthy! How nice to hear from you!" Grace Redmond's matronly voice drifted reassuringly over the wire.

"It's good to hear your voice too, Gram. Listen, I've got some time off and I was wondering if you'd care if I used the beach house."

Garth came right to the point, certain that his grandparents wouldn't object to the loan of the cottage.

"Well, of course you may use the cottage, dear. This is just wonderful! Your cousins are down there right now. If you can get there in the next couple of days, it'll give you a chance to visit with Dorothy, Frank, and the children."

Garth felt the tiny hairs on his neck bristle. Lord! Talk about topping off a rotten day. *Not Dorothy and Frank!* he pleaded silently. "They're using the cottage?" he asked.

"Yes, dear. Isn't it marvelous? They'll be there until . . . oh, dear, let me see . . . I believe until the day after tomorrow. When did you say your vacation started?"

Garth knew he couldn't tolerate two days locked inside a three-room cabin with his cousin Dorothy, her boastful husband Frank, and five of the rowdiest kids God had ever put on earth. He wasn't about to hurt Gram's feelings, but there was no way he was going anywhere near that cottage until Frank and Dorothy were gone.

"Gee, Gram, that sounds nice, but I'm afraid I can't make it before Sunday night. I guess by then Dorothy and the family will already have left."

Garth hated to lie, but he would if he had to.

"Oh, dear, I'm afraid they will have. Frank has to be at work on Monday. What a shame! Well, maybe you can visit with them next time," Grace said soothingly.

"Oh, sure thing. Tell them I'm sorry I'll miss them."

"Well, the key's under the mat, Garthy. Now, listen, you will come and see your grandma and grandpa before the winter's over, won't you? We'll be glad to send you a plane ticket."

Garth assured his grandmother that he'd

try to make the visit. He thanked her for the use of the cottage and hung up wondering what he would do for the next two days.

The thought of having to spend time in a hotel room wasn't pleasant, but it was his only choice. It beat having to tolerate good ol' hot-winded Frank and his five curtain climbers.

Hilary made a final swipe at her teary eyes as Garth finished his phone conversation. She promptly offered the return of his soiled handkerchief.

"Thanks . . . but just keep it." Garth told her.

"I'm sorry about the mascara. I think it'll come out in cold water," Hilary said, realizing why he was reluctant to accept it back.

"No, really, I don't need it," Garth replied. "Are you all right?"

"I'm fine, thank you."

Garth thought the woman looked as if someone had just shot her dog. Glancing around for the nearest lounge to wait out the layover, he eventually melted into the crowd as Hilary hobbled over to the waiting area and sat down.

Withdrawing a magazine from her purse, she began to read to pass the time until her plane left for West Creek. She had no idea what she would do when she got there, but she supposed she'd rent a cheap hotel room and try to rest a few days while she gathered her thoughts. Then she'd be forced to make the return trip home.

What was supposed to be a two-hour lay-over gradually dragged into eight. The lengthy delay didn't surprise her. In view of the past few hours, nothing surprised her.

Having purchased a fresh supply of Kleenex and a cup of hot chocolate around two o'clock, Hilary went back to her seat in the boarding area. By now, she was numb with fatigue, but her ankle didn't throb as much.

Garth spent the time in the lounge, eating bag after bag of corn chips. He had no idea why he was eating them. With his cold, he couldn't taste a thing. He supposed he was bored. The chaotic turn of events he'd encountered the last few hours had numbed him. He sneezed and reached into his pocket for another couple of antihistamines.

Around seven P.M., Flight 263 to West Creek was asked to begin boarding.

Garth boarded the plane last. He walked down the aisle, pausing before seat 3a in the nonsmoking section. He glanced down, and his heart sank. He saw the woman who'd been crying at the pay phone. She was sitting in the seat next to him.

"Hello again." Garth joined her and fastened the belt tightly around his waist. Damn! He hoped she wasn't going to bawl all the way to West Creek. He'd like to catch a few winks of sleep during the short flight.

"Oh . . . hello." Hilary sniffed and sat up straighter, wiping at her crimson-colored nose. She fought to stem the flow of tears.

Though the endless waterworks were beginning to wear on Garth's nerves, he was determined to be nice.

She was winsomely attractive—even if her eyes did look like two burnt holes in a blanket from all that crying. Shoulder-length dark brown hair framed her face in a soft cloud. Her eyes were a large watery blue, lined with spiky black lashes. She looked like a little pup that had just been kicked.

Under different circumstances Garth would have asked her name, but right now he was bone-weary. Socializing was the last thing on his mind.

"Are you all right?" He finally grumbled under his breath as he reached for the pamphlet the stewardess was holding up.

"Oh, yes. I'm . . . fine, thank you."

If this was fine, I'd hate to see her when something's really bothering her, Garth thought fleetingly.

Hilary realized she was making him nervous. He was just too polite to say anything. The poor man had been subjected to her blubbering long enough. He had to be getting a little tired of it. And he had been so nice, lending her his handkerchief and all. Hilary shut her eyes and drew a deep breath. She promised herself she would not think of Lenny Ricetrum. She would allow herself only pleasant thoughts.

"Magazine?" Garth offered, trying to take her mind off her troubles.

"No, thank you. I lost one of my contacts at the airport, and I can't see very well."

"Oh." Garth went back to riffling through the pages of the pamphlet. Hilary noticed that he suddenly paused and stared off into space. He glanced back at her, then quickly back down at the pamphlet.

"Did you lose your contact at this airport?" Garth asked in what he hoped sounded like a casual voice.

"Yes. Why?"

Garth grinned lamely. "Oh, no reason."

Tale of Love

Settling back comfortably in her seat, Hilary tried to concentrate on something pleasant.

Moments later she found herself focusing on the man sitting next to her. He was good-looking. Crisp, clean-cut—even though he could stand a shave. His hair was a pretty chestnut color, with red highlights, and his eyes were a nice doe-brown. The build beneath the leather jacket he was wearing was impressive.

He works out, Hilary decided. She turned her gaze back to the window as she caught him looking at her over the top of his magazine.

He wouldn't dump a girl without an explanation the way Lenny had, Hilary thought intuitively. Tears began rolling out of the corners of her eyes.

She fumbled in her purse for a clean tissue but discovered that, as usual, she didn't have one. A few minutes later Hilary heard a resigned sigh, and another snowy-white handkerchief magically appeared in her hand. *No,* she thought as she blew her nose for the hundredth time, *he wouldn't treat a girl that way.*

When the plane touched down in West

Creek, Hilary took her makeup kit straight to the ladies' room, where she applied fresh makeup and combed her hair. She was doing better. She hadn't shed a tear for almost thirty minutes, and she was optimistic that the crisis had finally passed.

Nearing the baggage pickup, Hilary witnessed a tender good-bye kiss shared by a young couple who were obviously in love. Her newly acquired "chin-up" attitude wavered, but she quickly diverted her attention and began looking for her luggage.

The revolving rack carouseled one fuzzy-looking suitcase after another past her blurred vision. Finally, Hilary thought she caught sight of two familiar pieces of Samsonite. She reached for the bags and was stunned when a large male hand hastily snaked in from behind her.

"Excuse me, but I believe this is my luggage," Garth apologized.

He groaned when he recognized her again.

Hilary turned to correct the mistaken intruder coolly. "I'm sorry, but I think you must be mistak—Oh, hello! It's you again!" Her face broke into a pleasant smile. "As I was saying, I think you must be mistaken. This is my luggage."

Garth returned her smile tolerantly. "No, I think you're mistaken. This is my luggage."

"Wait just a minute!" Suddenly Hilary had had it with being pushed around. She wasn't about to let this stranger take advantage of her, no matter how nice he'd been earlier. "This is my luggage, and I want you to let go of it!" she demanded.

"This can be settled easily enough." Garth stood his ground. "All we have to do is read the nametags. I'm sure you'll see you're mistaken. It's my luggage."

Hilary glanced around uneasily. The dispute was being closely watched by several other weary travelers eager to retrieve their own baggage. "Oh . . . yes, of course. That's the sensible thing to do."

Garth lifted the bags off the rack and carried them to the doorway. "Let's see what we have here." He silently read the first tag, and though he was disappointed to find it wasn't his, he found himself grinning devilishly. Glancing up at Hilary, he said solemnly, "I guess I was wrong. The bag isn't mine."

"I know." Hilary forced the smugness out of her voice. "That's what I've been trying to tell you."

Garth picked up the piece of luggage and

extended it to her courteously. "Here you go, Harry."

Hilary accepted the bag graciously, then frowned. "Harry?"

Garth lifted one brow questioningly. "You *are* Harry Hasseltine?"

"I certainly am not."

Garth grinned, displaying two of the most delightful dimples Hilary had ever seen. "You're not. That's too bad," he said dryly, "because this bag belongs to Harry Hasseltine."

"What? Let me see that!" Hilary felt her cheeks flush beet-red. On closer examination, Hilary discovered Garth was correct. The bags belonged to Harry Hasseltine. "What about the other one?" she challenged. Hilary thought she should know her own luggage.

Garth read the other tag. This time he was less pleased with the information it provided.

"Well?"

"Yours," he conceded humbly.

"I knew it!"

"Don't gloat."

Hilary forced herself not to. "Well, I suppose my other bag is still on the rack somewhere," she conceded.

They went back to the revolving rack and

waited until every single piece of luggage had been claimed. Their three bags failed to appear.

"Damn. There must have been a mix-up somewhere," Garth complained as he picked up her bag and they made their way to the baggage-claims department.

Garth noticed that Hilary was limping as they walked. "What's the matter with your foot?"

Color flooded Hilary's cheeks again. She'd hoped he wouldn't notice her swollen ankle. It strongly resembled an oversized soft ball now.

"I twisted my ankle earlier," she explained.

"That's too bad."

It took half an hour to inch their way to the claims window. They filled out the proper forms concerning lost luggage. Garth finished first and left a few minutes ahead of her. Hilary experienced a pang of disappointment as she watched him walk away. He'd been nice enough to ask if she needed help getting a cab. She'd gracefully declined his offer, and he'd left her leaning on the counter. He'd smiled at her and said, "Take it easy, Harry!"

When Hilary had completed her form she hobbled outside to summon a taxi. West

Creek's weather was considerably better than Raleigh's. The skies were overcast, but there was no sign of snow.

"Hi, again." Hilary set her bag down on the curb. She smiled at Garth, who was still trying to hail a cab.

"Hi. Get the forms filled out?"

"Yes. I hope it doesn't take long to locate the missing luggage."

"Me too. They have practically everything I own," Garth admitted.

Several cabs whizzed by before either Garth or Hilary could bring one to a halt. Garth finally made the first catch.

He opened the door and started to hop in, when he caught sight of Hilary standing on the curb, trying to balance on one leg. With a resigned grin, Garth slid back out of the cab and held the door open for her. "You take this one," he offered. He felt he owed her that much.

"Oh, no . . . please, I couldn't. You take it. I'll be fine."

"I insist."

"No, *I* insist."

Realizing they'd gone this route before with neither giving an inch, Garth gave in first to save time. "Look, if we don't decide

54

soon, the cab will leave without either one of us."

"I suppose we could share the ride," Hilary conceded. She could feel the exhaustion of the past few hours creeping up on her.

"Fine," Garth agreed. "I'll get your bags for you."

"Thanks." Hilary gratefully handed him her suitcase and makeup kit and limped over to the curb.

As the cab pulled away, Garth instructed the driver to take him to the West Creek Sheraton.

Hilary was grateful the driver assumed they both had the same destination. The hotel sounded terribly expensive to Hilary, who was quietly reassessing her limited funds, but perhaps if she were frugal, she could manage for a few days.

When the driver brought the taxi to a halt outside the Sheraton's elaborate front doors, Hilary knew she wasn't going to be able to afford the hotel.

Garth paid his fare and ducked out the door with a quick "Nice meeting you." The puzzled driver shot Hilary a questioning glance in the rearview mirror.

Hilary grinned back lamely. "Can you recommend a modestly priced hotel? One that's clean," she added quickly.

"Well, let's see . . . The Merrymont isn't bad. It's a nice family-type place about a mile on down the road."

"Thanks. The Merrymont will do nicely."

About the time Hilary's taxi had pulled up in front of the Merrymont, the management at the Sheraton was informing Garth that they had no available rooms. Had he booked even a day earlier, they could have accommodated him, they said with regret. But no rooms were vacant for tonight.

The manager offered to inquire about vacancies at other establishments, and Garth wearily thanked him. All he cared about was a bed that, hopefully, the roaches wouldn't carry off during the night.

After making several calls, the manager cheerfully informed Garth that he'd secured a room for him at the Merrymont.

"That's fine. How far is it?"

"Just down the road, sir. I'll get you a taxi."

When Hilary entered the Merrymont there were plenty of rooms. There was only one minor problem: The employees of the hotel had gone out on strike two hours earlier. The management assured her that, despite the inconvenience, they would extend every effort to make her stay as comfortable as possible.

"Would you phone the airport for me?" Hilary asked a clerk as she signed the register. "The airline has misplaced one of my bags. As soon as they're able to locate it, I'd like to have it sent directly to my room."

"Yes, ma'am. Your room is 402, and we hope you enjoy your stay." The inexperienced young desk clerk made a wholehearted attempt at professionalism as he handed her the key.

At this point, Hilary didn't care if they put her on the sofa in the lobby. She had to rest her ankle.

"Where are the elevators, please?"

"Oh . . . uh . . . sorry, ma'am. That's another little difficulty we're experiencing. The elevators are out of order right now, but we've called a repairman. He's due anytime. I'm sure he'll have them running in a jiffy. If you'd like to wait in the lobby, you're certainly welcome to do so."

Hilary looked at him in disbelief. "No, thanks. I'll take the stairs."

She silently thanked the airlines for losing

her other bag as she limped up four flights of stairs, lugging the makeup kit and dragging the heavy suitcase along behind her.

When she reached the fourth floor she sagged against the wall, gasping for breath. Her heartbeat had to be at least two hundred and sixty-five. She never realized how miserably out of shape she was.

Working her way down the dimly lit hallway, she found her room—the one farthest from the stairway. Hilary unlocked the door, flicked on the lamp, and fell across the bed in exhaustion. It was several moments before she could will herself to get up off the bed and close the door.

Sinking back on the bed, she surveyed the room and found it to be clean and adequately furnished.

A half hour later Hilary finally rolled off the side of the bed and went in search of the bathroom. The thought of soaking her ankle in a nice hot tub had become her newest priority.

With the tub brimming, its tantalizing warmth inviting, Hilary was mere inches away from submerging her throbbing ankle in the healing waters when a sharp rap at the door sounded.

She groaned and grabbed for the side of the tub. "Who is it?"

The rap sounded again, and she reluctantly reached for her robe. Seconds later she hobbled to the door.

"Yes?" Hilary called from behind the dead bolt.

Silence reigned supreme now.

She waited a few moments, then slid the bolt out of place and eased the door open cautiously.

Sitting before her were three pieces of blue Samsonite.

Realizing that only one could be hers, Hilary stepped into the hall to stop the bellhop. Whoever was responsible for their delivery, however, was long gone by now.

She knelt down to squint at the tags and found that one of the bags was indeed hers. The other two belonged to a Mr. Garth Redmond . . . whoever he might be.

Hilary sighed and began to drag the luggage into the room. She closed the door and went back in the bathroom. When she was through with her bath, she'd call the desk and inform the clerk of the error. As far as Hilary was concerned, Garth Redmond was going to be without luggage for another hour.

Chapter Four

HILARY LAY IN THE TUB AND soaked the injured ankle for more than an hour. She finally summoned enough energy to dry off and apply cream and powder. She was relieved to have her personal articles back in her possession. She decided that the bath had been just the thing to cheer her up.

Her gaze caught the two pieces of Samsonite still sitting beside the bed. Garth what's-his-name would probably appreciate having his possessions, Hilary conceded with a pang of guilt. She should have reported the mistake earlier.

The teenybopper who was manning the front desk answered her call in a California Valley–voice that Hilary found difficult to decipher.

"Yoah! What is it?" The exuberant greeting caught Hilary off guard. The teen's voice was undergoing rapid adolescent changes. Hilary wasn't sure what he'd said, much less what he'd meant.

"Yes . . . this is Hilary Brookfield in Room 402. Two pieces of luggage have been delivered to my room by mistake."

"No joke?"

"Yes, no joke. Would you please send someone to get them?"

"Sure thing, lady. Do they have a name on 'em?"

"Yes. They belong to Garth Redmond."

"Redmond, Redmond . . ." The young man repeated the name. Hilary could hear him frantically rummaging through his registration forms.

"Yeah, here ya go . . . Garth Redmond. He's in Room 404. Uh, sorry 'bout the mix-up there, lady. Tell ya what I'm gonna do. Soon as

I can put a fix on that bellhop guy, I'll send him up to get 'em."

Hilary thought of the hour she'd already wasted. Mr. Redmond would want to have his personal toiletries as soon as possible. Since he was next door, Hilary decided to deliver the bags herself. She'd bet dollars to doughnuts that Mr. Redmond was a kindly old gent who would deeply appreciate her act of kindness.

Besides, there was the staff strike to consider. The few employees the hotel had managed to recruit were inexperienced and, understandably, overworked. With the elevator still on the blink, the least Hilary could do was offer to help.

"If it isn't against hotel policy, I could set Mr. Redmond's luggage outside his door," she said.

"Lady I don't know nothin' about no hotel policy—know what I mean? But if you're sure it wouldn't be too much of a hassle, hop to it." The clerk accepted her offer eagerly.

"All right," Hilary said. "I'll take care of it immediately."

"Gee, thanks a wad, lady."

Hilary hurriedly dressed, then gathered the luggage. Gingerly placing her weight on the injured ankle, she smiled when she discovered that the pain was tolerable. Adding just a fraction more of her weight, she suddenly winced and cried out in pain. The injury was better but far from healed. Hilary didn't need to remind herself a second time to keep most of her weight off that ankle.

Talk about weight! Hilary complained to herself as she grunted and tugged the two bulging suitcases to the door. *Poor old Mr. Redmond must have packed his respirator in one of these things!*

Hilary toyed with the idea of knocking on the door of Room 404 and abandoning the baggage. That's how hers had been delivered. Then she decided against it.

If Mr. Redmond is in ill health, she told herself, *he won't be able to manage the bags by himself.* By now Hilary had convinced herself that Garth Redmond was a senior citizen. He could even be napping and not hear the knock on the door. The bags could be stolen before Mr. Redmond realized they'd even been returned. Hilary decided to knock on the door and assist with the heavy luggage. She tapped lightly, allowing ample time for the aging man to respond.

Mr. Redmond would appreciate her thoughtfulness, Hilary told herself again. And it would be nice to hear a man say thank you, for a change. Her morale could use the boost. *Perhaps he's hard of hearing,* Hilary thought as she rapped a second time.

Garth rolled over on the bed and tried to clear his mind. Lack of sleep and the multitude of cold pills he'd been taking were making him so groggy he could hardly wake up. Was someone trying to beat the door down, or was he dreaming?

Annoyed and still half asleep, Garth rolled out of bed as the knock sounded again. He stumbled toward the door, grumbling under his breath about never being able to get any rest, when his big toe found the straight pin that had been carelessly dropped on the carpeted floor by the last occupant of the room.

"Oh, damn!" Garth sucked in his breath and dropped to one knee as he tried to identify the object that had just harpooned him. A moment later he gingerly plucked the pin from his throbbing toe. The trickle of blood that oozed from the tiny prick made him feel light-headed. Garth had never been able to stand the sight of blood—especially not his own.

A third knock on the door brought him to his feet again, and he hurried across the room.

"Okay! Okay! Don't knock the thing off its hinges!" Garth shouted irritably. He undid the lock and opened the door a fraction.

Hilary saw one blazing eye peering back at her. "Mr. Redmond? I'm sorry to bother you, but—oh, hi there!" Hilary was shocked yet delighted to see the man from the airport standing in the doorway.

Garth finally managed to focus his bleary gaze on the person standing in the doorway.

It was her again.

"My goodness, what a surprise!" Hilary exclaimed.

"Yeah . . . How you doing?" Garth tried to remain civil as every bone in his body cried for mercy.

"Well, how do you like that! I thought you were an old man!" she said brightly.

"A what?" Garth sagged against the doorframe, wondering where she got her energy. He knew she had been up all night crying, but she looked as fresh as a daisy. He envied her stamina.

"Are *you* Garth Redmond?"

"I was a few hours ago. I'm not too sure right now."

"Well, I'm Hilary Brookfield. I thought you were staying at the Sheraton. What happened?"

"They didn't have any vacancies." Garth yawned.

"Well, guess what?" Hilary exclaimed.

"I haven't the faintest."

"I have a surprise."

Garth caught himself swaying forward as he felt his energy draining. "You were banging on my door to tell me you have a surprise?" He couldn't believe the woman. "Couldn't it have waited until later?"

"Yes, but I thought you'd want to know right away. Of course, I didn't know *you* were Garth Redmond, or I wouldn't have bothered you until you had rested a while . . ."

Noting his cool indifference, Hilary felt her lower lip begin to quiver, a warning sign Garth had come to recognize and fear. He was acting as if she were bothering him instead of doing him a favor, Hilary thought resentfully.

The ungrateful clod! She'd only wanted to help. All she'd gotten for her efforts was a sarcastic You were banging on my door to tell me that? It wasn't fair.

Hilary's injured pride ballooned as she recalled every injustice fate had dealt her in the past twenty-four hours—most of which she considered undeserved.

No one appreciated her. No one. Not Lenny Ricetrum—he'd dumped her for a redhead. Not Marsha—she'd deserted her for Jamaica. A strong wave of self-pity flooded over Hilary, and lack of sleep was not adding to her usual good disposition.

Hilary told herself that she was one giant doormat for the whole world to wipe their dirty feet on. Not even Mr. O'Connor appreciated her, she concluded. If the truth were known, he'd probably agreed to the unscheduled vacation just to get her out of the office.

And now, this . . . this *ingrate* didn't even appreciate the effort it took for her to deliver his missing luggage—in person. What did he care that she had a swollen ankle, was blind in one eye, not to mention that she was still in shock from having had her heart ripped right out of her chest!

The list could go on forever and the disinterested look on Garth Redmond's face was the last straw! She began to cry again.

Garth suddenly came to life. He flung open

the door and pointed his finger sternly in her direction. "Don't start that again," he warned. He knew that once she was wound up the tears wouldn't stop for hours.

"I bothered you to return your luggage, Mr. Redmond! I was 'banging' on your door because I thought you might appreciate having clean clothes." Hilary stiffened her lower lip defensively. "I can see I was mistaken."

Garth glanced down, and he saw the two bags sitting at her feet. "Oh . . . well . . . thanks." He felt like a heel for shouting at her.

"Thanks?"

Garth bristled at the sharp accusation in her voice. "Yes, thanks! I appreciate it!" Lord, what did the woman want? Blood?

"Well, all I can say is, if I had known they were your bags, I wouldn't have put myself out to deliver them," Hilary declared.

"I said I appreciate it. Do you want me to get down on my knees and say it again?"

"That won't be necessary . . . but do you realize the elevator's out," Hilary reminded him.

"You carried the bags up four flights of stairs?" Garth didn't know why she had his bags or why she would want to carry them up

four flights of stairs on a twisted ankle, just to bring them to him.

Hilary refused to answer. He could come to whatever conclusion he wanted. She hadn't carried the bags up four flights of stairs, but she was feeling just neglected and irritated enough to let him think she had.

"All right," Garth conceded. "I appreciate your delivering the bags, okay? I was half asleep, and I didn't mean to snap at you." He'd feel awful if anyone had seen her dragging his luggage up the stairs—at least anyone who could connect the bags to him. She couldn't weigh more than a hundred pounds soaking wet . . . And with that twisted ankle . . . Garth flinched.

"I accept your apology, and you can rest assured I'll not be bothering you again," Hilary promised. She was still visibly miffed at what she considered his bad manners. She turned and began to hobble back to her room.

"You staying here?"

The slamming of a door gave Garth his answer; she was right next door.

Garth glanced around, feeling that he was being watched. He noted the piercing surveillance of a middle-aged woman across the hall. Her dark eyes impaled him from behind her half-opened door, and it was evident that she'd monitored the whole conversation.

"Look, I'm sorry," Garth apologized. He turned his palms up helplessly. "I didn't ask her to bring my luggage. Okay?"

The woman, whose hair was wrapped tightly in pink curlers, gave him a nasty look before she slammed her door shut as well.

When Hilary returned to her room she flung herself across the bed. The unnerving encounter with Garth Redmond had only served to remind her of how alone she was. She buried her face in the depths of the pillow and wished she had never made this miserable trip. It was just another harrowing episode on her growing list of mistakes.

Feeling a stab of homesickness, Hilary considered returning to Denver on the next available flight. Obviously she wasn't going to be able to forget Lenny. A week's vacation would have been nice, but with Marsha gone, it seemed pointless.

Hilary felt that she might as well go home and face the problem head on. It wouldn't be pleasant, but she was sure she would survive. She decided to rest just a few minutes before she called the airport . . .

* * *

Giving the woman across the hall a mental raspberry, Garth picked up the two bags and carried them into his room.

He realized he'd been sharp with . . . what was the girl's name? Hilda . . . Holly . . . Heidi? He couldn't remember, but he regretted having made her cry again.

The woman had problems, but so did he. Garth absentmindedly touched the heavy stubble on his face. What he needed was a shower, a shave, and twenty-four hours of undisturbed sleep.

The shower worked like a shot of adrenaline. Garth shaved, then dressed, but his conscience still nagged him.

Maybe he should step next door and thank the girl again for bringing his luggage. Garth shook his head admiringly. *Four* flights of stairs! With a twisted ankle, dragging two bags that weighed as much as she did!

The woman had guts.

Garth knew he would sleep better if he checked on her first. He sighed, slapped on a musky-smelling aftershave, combed his hair, and quickly left the room.

He tapped softly on the door of Room 402, praying that the woman in the pink curlers across the hall wouldn't hear him. He waited several minutes before he tapped again. Still no response.

Well, so much for chivalry, Garth thought as he turned to go back to his room. Heidi was probably down in the bar having a drink; she must have forgotten all about the incident.

As Garth entered his room again he hung the Do not disturb sign on the doorknob outside. Seconds later he climbed wearily back into bed. For the next forty-eight hours he was going to do what he'd been sent here to do: Relax.

Chapter Five

STARTLED BY SHOUTS AND POUND-
ing on doors, Garth sat bolt upright in bed.
Fighting off the cobwebs of a deep sleep, he
shook his head several times. He tried to focus
his vision. *Now* what was going on, he wondered irritably.

If he'd felt annoyed at the earlier interrup-
tion, Garth was inclined to be furious this
time. He had been so tired that it had taken
him an hour to relax and finally doze off.

Garth was sure he couldn't have slept more

than a moment, even if the clock on the night-stand told him otherwise. He had slept for at least ten hours. It was morning now, almost six-thirty A.M.

Grabbing the rumpled sheet, Garth gave it a good jerk and tossed it aside. His feet hit the floor at the same time a loud knock sounded at his door. He grabbed his pants off the back of a chair.

If Heidi was back again, he'd personally strangle her, he vowed as he fumbled for his shoes. Mumbling a few choice threats under his breath, he searched frantically under the bed for the missing mate. He wasn't going to take the chance of being harpooned again.

There was another sharp rap at the door, followed by a man's voice. "Open up!" he shouted.

Garth retrieved the missing shoe as another sudden loud thump at the door sent his head banging into the frame of the bed.

"Damn!" Garth ran his tongue over his bleeding lip as he clutched the shoe and crawled to freedom.

Rubbing the goose egg–sized lump that was beginning to rise on top of his head, he hopped to the door while trying to put his shoe on at the same time. He jerked the door open, vowing to take revenge on the knuckle-head responsible for the invasion of his privacy. Garth was totally unprepared to see a fireman standing in his doorway.

"Yes?"

"Sorry to disturb you, sir, but we're going to have to ask you to vacate the building."

He noted the man's fire-fighting gear. The man stood, ax in hand, in the hallway reeking now with thick foul-smelling smoke. Coughing, Garth had a sinking feeling that this wasn't a fire drill.

As if his nerves weren't already dangling by threads! The thought of being fried alive didn't help the situation any!

"Oh, hell!" Garth turned four shades paler. "What's going on?"

Recognizing the panic etched on Garth's face, the fireman tried to calm him down. "We have a small fire here on the fourth floor, sir. We're asking all the guests to vacate the premises immediately."

"Ah . . . yeah . . . sure. I just need to get my things first." Garth whirled around when the man's sharp rebuttal stopped him.

"Leave them!"

"But—"

"Look, mister, right now we've got this

thing under control. But it's possible that could change."

"Oh . . . yeah. I'm going."

"Take the stairs at the end of the hall, buddy. *Don't* use the elevator!" The fireman warned. Then he continued down the hall to alert the other guests.

Moving in a daze, Garth headed for the end of the hallway. As he passed Room 402 the door flew open, and Hilary came rushing out. She was clutching something to her chest.

Garth noticed she was wearing her nightie. "Are you still here?" He realized that the fireman should have knocked on the door of 402 before banging on his.

"I had to go back for my makeup," Hilary said breathlessly.

"Your *what?*"

"My makeup." She looked at Garth guiltily. "I look terrible without it . . ." Her lame reply was drowned out by the harsh demands of the fireman shouting.

"Hey, you two! Out of the building. *Now!*"

Garth took Hilary firmly by the arm and propelled her toward the stairway. "Come on, we have to take the stairs!" As he opened the door to the stairway he drew her back protectively into his arms when he saw the cloud of thick smoke blocking the fire exit. "We can't take the stairs," he said needlessly.

"Oh, my gosh! What'll we do?" Garth could feel Hilary trembling as he drew her closer to him.

"Come on." Garth grabbed her hand and pulled Hilary along behind him. Remembering her injured ankle, Garth finally stopped and scooped her up in his arms, then raced down the hall to the outside fire escape.

As he stepped onto the metal steps, a gust of frigid air rippled up the back of the thin shirt he wearing.

"I wish you'd brought a coat while you were at it," Garth bantered, trying to ease the look of horror on Hilary's face. He felt her arms tighten around his neck more securely.

"What's wrong?"

Wide-eyed, Hilary shook her head. "No . . . I can't . . ." She was looking down, shaking her head, her arms wrapped around his neck so tightly he could barely breathe.

"Oh, yes, *we* can," Garth assured her, trying to loosen the stranglehold she had on his throat.

Too petrified to speak, Hilary fervently shook her head, no!

"Just hold on. I'll carry you down—"

"Down? On, no! You can't . . ." she pleaded. "I'm terrified of heights!"

Heights! Garth thought. *It's not as though we're on top of the Eiffel Tower, for crying out loud!* Seeing fresh tears surfacing in her eyes, Garth sighed.

"And I'm not overly fond of being burned alive," he said, "so let's compromise. You shut your eyes and don't look down, and I'll get us out of here before the whole building goes up in flames."

With a horrified gasp, Hilary buried her face in his neck. "I'm scared, Garth."

"I'm scared too," he admitted. "Just hold on."

She nodded. "Please walk slowly."

"It depends on how hot it gets." Garth hefted her up more comfortably in his arms, then began to ease his way down the metal stairway.

The wind was gusty, and it was getting colder. The streets below were teeming with activity as sirens wailed and flashing red lights lit up the darkened sky.

"It's all right. We're only four floors up. It's really not that high." He encouraged her as he took each step slowly. He was careful to keep his voice calm as he cautiously wound his way around the narrow staircase. Heights were not exactly Garth's favorite thing either, and the small patches of ice he encountered occasionally on the steps were not exactly comforting.

"Are you all right?"

"Are we almost down?"

"Not quite. Three floors to go."

"Three!"

"You're doing fine. Don't look down."

"I'm not looking in any direction."

It wasn't until his feet had touched solid ground that Hilary stopped shaking and she dared to open her eyes.

The impact of what was happening finally hit her like a ton of bricks.

"Oh, my gosh! What about my clothes? I'm not even dressed!"

Shivering with cold, Garth set her on her feet. "I don't know. We'll have to see how bad the fire turns out to be. The fireman talked as if they had it under control."

Volunteers from the Red Cross hurried over to drape warm blankets around their shoulders. Cups of hot coffee were placed in their hands, and they gratefully sipped as they were pushed aside by the milling crowd.

They wandered across the street and sat

down on the curb, drinking the coffee and staring up at the fourth floor where all their personal belongings were.

"There's an awful lot of smoke coming out of those windows," Hilary observed.

"Not that much. You know how safety-conscious hotels are. They'll have us back in our rooms in a few hours at the most," Garth predicted.

As he spoke, angry flames began to belch out of several windows on the fourth floor.

"Oh, dear," Hilary winced. "I think we've had it."

Had it they had.

The fire developed into a major one. While Garth and Hilary sat and sipped coffee, the entire fourth and fifth floors of the hotel went up in flames.

Every stitch of clothing they had brought with them, except for the few pieces they had on their backs, burned before their eyes.

Garth took the disaster with resignation. "You know, Heidi—"

"It's Hilary," she corrected him. "Hilary Brookfield."

"Oh, I'm sorry. I've been trying to remember," Garth apologized. "Anyway, as I was saying, I've had one hell of a twenty-four hours. What about you?"

Hilary nodded. "Miserable! And I came here to get away from it all!"

Garth looked at her and began to chuckle. A deep, nice sound. One that brought an immediate smile to Hilary's face. "You too?"

They both broke out into laughter, relieving the tension that had been building for hours.

"Well . . ." Garth leaned his elbows back on the curb when their amusement finally subsided. He stared up at the burning fourth and fifth floors of the hotel. "Things could be worse. Material possessions can be replaced. At least no lives were lost."

Hilary had to agree. He was right . . . It could have been much worse.

"Wonder how it started?"

"I heard someone say a man was smoking in bed."

"That's sad."

"Well . . ." Garth yawned and stretched lazily. "I don't know about you, but I could use something to eat. Are you hungry?" He smiled, determined to make the best out of a bad situation.

Hilary realized that she hadn't eaten a

thing in the last twenty-four hours. "Yes, I'm starved."

Having spotted a small diner across the street earlier, they wandered away from the scene of the fire.

"I shouldn't go in looking like this," Hilary fretted. She clutched the blanket more tightly around her chin.

"No one will care," Garth promised. He ushered her into the warmth of the small building. It was almost deserted; everyone was watching the fire.

The menu didn't offer a large selection, but after pondering the choices they settled for grilled cheese sandwiches and Cokes.

Sharing a broken-down booth, they ate the meal slowly, savoring the warmth of the diner as they watched the frenzied activity outside.

Eventually the conversation drifted to the reason they were both in West Creek, and once more Hilary felt the hot sting of tears.

Garth glanced up from his plate expectantly, surprised to see that she was crying again. "Hey, what are the tears for? I thought we agreed we were pretty lucky."

"Oh, it isn't the fire . . ." Hilary fumbled for a tissue, waving one hand dismissively as she blew her nose. "Just ignore me. It'll pass in a minute."

"Look . . ." Garth reached in his pocket and retrieved the handkerchief she had used earlier. He handed it to her. "I've watched you crying for twenty-four hours. I don't know what's wrong, but it surely can't be all that bad."

"But it is," she sobbed, burying her face in the handkerchief for another good cry. "I've been dumped!"

"Dumped?" Garth looked at her blankly. *Dumped. What was that supposed to mean?*

When the tears finally subsided, Hilary found herself telling Garth about her recent breakup with Lenny, the harrowing ride to the airport, how she'd twisted her ankle, lost a contact, and Marsha's unexpected exit to Jamaica.

Instead of dismissing her troubles as minor and unworthy of such a concentration of despair, Garth was surprisingly understanding.

"I know how you feel," he admitted. "The reason I'm here is because my boss thinks I'm stressed out."

"Well, I thought I had stress before," Hilary confessed, trying to find a dry spot on the handkerchief to blow her nose. "But since I left Denver, it's been Trauma City."

Garth nodded. "I know." It hadn't exactly been Christmas morning for him either. "Well, look"—Garth reached over to take her hand supportively—"It's been rough, but the worst is over. As soon as we can, we'll look for new accommodations, and then we'll both get that rest we came for."

"Yes, I suppose so."

Funny, Hilary would have thought that a man holding her hand would upset her so soon after Lenny. Instead, she found the unexpected gesture comforting. Garth had nice hands, large and protective. For the first time in hours, Hilary felt the world beginning to turn right side up again.

"Do you have any idea what you're planning to do, now that your friend is in Jamaica?" Garth asked.

"I was planning on taking the next flight home—before the fire." Hilary surveyed her bathrobe dismally. "Now, I don't know. I'll have to have clothes before I get on a plane."

"Well, I suppose we can—" Garth's words were severed in midsentence as he felt a steel hand clamp down on his shirt collar. He glanced up, and his eyes widened as he was

jerked out of the booth by the scruff of his
neck.

"What the—" Garth yelled as a man twice
his size—twice anyone's size—dangled him in
the air by his collar. The intruder glared at
Garth as if he were about to disassemble him
—piece by piece.

The burly character looked Garth squarely
in the eye without blinking and stated in a
voice that sounded like creek gravel, "The
question is, what do *you* think you're doing,
chump!"

By now Garth was red-faced and gasping
for breath. He was clearly in no condition to
answer the man's question.

"Hey! You want to put me down!" Garth
finally managed to wheeze out. He had no
idea who this maniac was or what he'd done
to antagonize him. The only thing he *was* sure
of was that he had no intention of provoking
him further.

Like a bolt of lightening, Hilary sprang to
her one good foot. "You put him *down* this
instant!" she demanded. "Who do you think
you are?"

*Oh, please, Hilary don't get him any mad-
der!* Garth willed silently as he watched her
go nose-to-nose with the giant.

"I'm warning you! *Put him down!*" Hilary threatened. She snapped her fingers, then pointed at the giant authoritatively.

Maybe she knows karate, Garth prayed. His face was beginning to turn a splotchy blue. No, even if she knew karate, kung fu and had a Sears, Roebuck chain saw in the pocket of her bathrobe, Garth realized, she still was no match for this bonzo burger.

To Garth's astonishment, Hilary got her point across. The giant dropped Garth like a sack of grain, and he fell limply into the booth as the man confronted Hilary, still eye-to-eye.

Garth began sucking in deep gulps of air as Hilary spoke to the bully curtly. "Just what do you think you're doing?"

"I came looking for you, babe." The man's deep voice had suddenly taken on a tone of boyish pleading as he stepped forward and tried to take Hilary in his arms.

"Wait a minute!" Garth moved to protect Hilary, but she gently pushed him back down in the booth.

"It's all right," she said. "I'll take care of this."

"Are you sure?" Garth was confident there wasn't a lot he could do anyway—given the hundred-pound difference in size between himself and the giant—but he was willing to try.

"How did you know where to find me?" Hilary asked calmly, ignoring Garth's struggle to get to his feet again.

Garth had a tight feeling in the pit of his stomach, coinciding with the one he still had around his neck. All he'd ever heard about "a lover scorned" came rushing back to him. This undoubtedly must be "the rat," Lenny Ricetrum.

"I called the boss, and he said you'd gone to West Creek to spend some time with a girlfriend. Some girlfriend!" Lenny sneered. He glanced at Garth disdainfully, then back to Hilary and demanded, "Where's your clothes?"

"On the fourth floor of that burning hotel!"

Lenny shot a hurried glance out of the window. Assured that she was telling him the truth, his scowl began to slowly recede.

"Mr. O'Connor told *you* where I was?" Hilary demanded.

"Well, not me exactly. I had a friend call. Jake told Michael that he was your cousin from out of town," Lenny admitted.

It infuriated Hilary to think that Lenny had

stooped to such low-down tactics. Especially after having treated her so badly.

"I realized I made a mistake, babe." Lenny smiled at her persuasively. "I came all this way just so we could patch things up."

"Oh, what a shame! Did you bring the little redhead too?" Hilary asked pleasantly.

Garth found it hard to believe that this was the man Hilary had wept through three boxes of Kleenex for. Lenny didn't appear to be her type.

"I don't want the redhead, Hilary. I want you," Lenny admitted contritely. He tapped a tightly clenched fist against his leg and shot Garth another nasty look. His voice dropped repentantly. "I made a mistake, okay?"

"Well, Lenny, we all make mistakes, but I'm afraid this one can't be corrected that easily," Hilary told him.

Reconciling with Lenny? After he had treated her so shabbily? Hilary realized that was something she was going to have to think about.

"Come on, honey," Lenny coaxed. "Let's go somewhere and talk this thing over." He shot Garth another warning look.

Hilary looked at Garth, then back at Lenny.

"Go ahead. Don't worry about me," Garth

offered, hoping they would leave him out of it.

Hilary realized she was about to do a devious thing, but she needed time to think. She just hoped Garth would play along.

"No, I don't think so. I'm here for vacation, and I'm staying." She slid in the booth next to Garth and slipped her arm through his. "With Garth."

Garth's eyes widened.

Lenny's upper lip curled ominously as his snapping black eyes openly accused Garth of trifling with his woman.

"I thought you were going to take the next plane," Garth reminded Hilary as he casually removed her arm from his.

Garth liked Hilary, and he would have helped her out if he could have. But he wasn't prepared to lose his life for her.

"I'm staying!" Hilary said. She firmly linked her arm back with his.

"Now, look"—Garth was beginning to lose his patience—"I don't want to get involved in this . . ."

Lenny's face resembled an approaching cloudburst. "Well, well, well! Ain't this cozy! You work fast, buddy boy!"

"No, this isn't what you think." Garth tried

to explain, but Hilary was doing nothing to help. In fact, she seemed to be deliberately egging him on. "Tell him, Hilary . . ."

"Tell him what?" Hilary asked unconcernedly. She picked up the menu to study it.

"Tell him why we happen to be together." Garth decided to be firm with her. "Right now! I've grown fond of my neck!"

Lenny looked as if he were ready to blow a fuse.

"Leave Garth alone, Lenny. You're making him nervous," Hilary said obediently.

"Are you coming with me, or are you staying here with this jerk?" Lenny demanded. He was getting tired of begging. Lenny Ricetrum had never begged a woman in his life, and he sure wasn't about to start now.

Hilary carefully placed the menu back on the rack. "I'm staying with the jerk," she announced.

"Now just a minute . . ." Garth said resentfully.

Hilary patted Garth's arm reassuringly. "Go away, Lenny. Garth and I want to be alone."

Garth was dismayed. Every word Hilary said was clearly designed to give the erroneous impression that he and she were together.

Really *together!* Garth had the growing suspicion that Lenny Ricetrum planned to squeeze him to death . . . slowly and painfully.

Hilary's reaction left Garth bewildered and just a little irritated. He had enough trouble without having an irate boyfriend on his tail. Not only was Hilary deliberately aggravating a man who weighed twice what Garth did, she seemed to be enjoying it!

The sound of a meaty fist crashing down on the table convinced Garth that Lenny was aware of the goading.

"Look, Ricetrum. I haven't moved in on your territory, but if the lady doesn't want to go with you, she doesn't want to go," Garth said. He stood up to face his adversary, trying to remember if he had ever made out a will.

Garth winced as the meaty fist hit the table a second time, rattling the dishes loudly again.

"Hey, you, back there! What are you trying to do, tear down the joint?" The proprietor of the diner shouted. "Either put a lid on it, or take it down the street!"

Thank God! reinforcements! Garth's knees sagged with relief. He'd wondered just how long the owner would continue to keep his eyes glued to the football game on the portable black-and-white television set.

Lenny eyed Garth coldly. Hilary glared at Lenny with a look that could freeze hell over, and Garth wished to high heaven he'd never left Chicago.

"Well, you and ol' lover boy better watch your step," Lenny warned, deciding to let the matter lie for the moment. "But let me warn you, sweetheart, you'd better reconsider."

Garth put his arm around Hilary protectively. "Why don't you bug off, Ricetrum. Can't you see the lady's not interested?"

Garth's eyes suddenly bulged as Lenny pulled him up again and jerked the collar of his shirt into a tight knot, choking off his breath once more.

"Hilary, dammit! Tell him you'll at least think about it!" Garth gasped.

"Never," Hilary stated calmly.

"You better hope she gives it another thought, sucker. You'd just better hope she does!"

Lenny dropped Garth back down onto his feet, pivoted on the ball of his foot, and marched out of the restaurant angrily.

Garth grabbed his swollen neck and fell back in the booth limply.

He shot Hilary a murderous look as she sat calmly sucking up what was left of her Coke through a straw.

Stress? Joel Anderson had thought Garth was suffering from stress before? He should see him now.

Chapter Six

"OKAY, YOU WANT TO TELL ME what *that* was all about."

Garth was still shaken by the events of the past five minutes. From the moment he'd first laid eyes on Hilary, he'd wondered if she wasn't an apple short of being a bushel.

Now he strongly suspected she was—and it was beginning to look as if she were harboring a silent death wish for him.

Rubbing his aching throat, Garth waited

while Hilary nervously twisted her straw into the shape of distressed pretzel.

"That was Lenny—the man I told you about."

"I just about had that figured out."

Guiltily, Hilary dropped her eyes away from Garth's. "I should have warned you. Lenny has a nasty temper."

"I noticed that right away too. What I didn't notice was that we were together—I mean, as in *personally* together!" Garth challenged.

Hilary hung her head sheepishly. "Oh, that . . . Well, I had to think fast. I'm sorry I involved you, but I knew Lenny would insist I return to Denver with him . . . and I don't want to."

"You don't want to!" Garth shook his head in disbelief. "I thought that's what all the waterworks were about."

"Yes . . . but I need time to think." Hilary deposited the mangled straw in the ashtray. "Lenny needs to be taught a lesson. He can't just up and dump me, then waltz back into my life as if nothing happened." She had a little pride left.

"Fine! But from now on, pick another guinea pig," Garth warned. He reached for the check. "I came here looking for a little peace and quiet, and I don't plan to get involved in a lover's spat."

"Lenny isn't my lover," Hilary stated flatly.

"Well, he sure isn't mine!"

Hilary's face suddenly softened. "I'm sorry, Garth . . . really."

"It's okay . . . And I don't want you to take this personally, but I think it's time we went our separate ways." Garth didn't mean to sound harsh, yet he felt it imperative to let her know where he stood. Fate had thrown them together constantly, but the time had come to part.

"Oh, I don't take it personally," Hilary assured him. "I think you're right . . . and I'm sorry about involving you the way I did. It won't happen again."

Garth straightened his collar petulantly, wincing when the material rubbed his bruised neck. "It's all right . . . but don't do it again."

"I wouldn't think of it." Hilary slid out of the booth and reached for the check. "Please, I insist on paying."

"That isn't necessary," Garth said dismissively. "I'll get it." He reached over and absentmindedly tucked the blanket up closer around her neck. "You're . . . uh . . .

you're showing too much . . ." Garth was finding it increasingly hard to keep his eyes off the tantalizing sight of the soft swell of creamy flesh the blanket was doing an inadequate job of concealing.

"Oh," Hilary glanced down, wondering exactly how much of her "uh's" had been exposed. "Thank you."

"You're welcome." *She sure has some figure,* Garth thought. He ran his eyes lazily over her petite form, which was draped enchantingly in the dark blanket. No wonder Ricetrum had blown his cool.

"About the check . . . I really wish you'd let me pay," Hilary persisted as she reached for her purse.

"It's not necessary," Garth repeated. He didn't want to stand there all night and argue over four dollars and twenty-eight cents.

"But I want to," Hilary insisted, and Garth found himself returning her smile.

He reached over and ruffled her hair goodnaturedly. She had pretty hair, thick and lustrous. "I'll get the check," he stated firmly.

"You've been awfully nice about all of this." With a sparkle in her eyes that Garth found disturbingly appealing, Hilary reached for her makeup kit, and the blanket slipped a notch lower. She glanced up and smiled guiltily as Garth quickly averted his eyes. She tugged the blanket primly back in place.

"Oh, dear!"

"What now?" Garth noticed she was looking askance at the makeup kit.

"My purse . . . it's still in the hotel room."

"You mean you saved the makeup kit and left your purse?" He found that sort of feminine behavior hard to comprehend.

Hilary nodded miserably. "It had my plane ticket and all my money in it."

"Oh, bother!" Garth swore under his breath, realizing what her loss could mean.

She lifted her eyes hopefully. "What do you think I should do?"

"I don't know." Garth wasn't sure what *he* was going to do, but he knew one thing: He wasn't in any shape to be responsible for her too. "I'll take care of the check; then we'll try to figure out something."

"Thanks . . . I'll pay you back."

While he was paying the cashier, Hilary tried to decide what to do next. She couldn't expect Garth to take care of her. They barely knew each other, and he had made it clear that he was in West Creek for complete relax-

101

ation. He had been wonderful to her, but she couldn't continue to impose upon him.

She would have to call her parents and ask them to wire money, but she realized even that could take time. What was she to do in the meantime?

Garth returned from the cashier. They stood for a moment. He smiled lamely, and she smiled back.

Garth barely knew her, yet he couldn't just leave her sitting in a diner wrapped in a blanket. But if he took her with him, he'd never get any rest. Her luck seemed to be as incredibly rotten as his.

"Do you know anyone else in West Creek you can call?"

"No." Hilary shook her head sadly. "I'll have to call my parents and have them wire me some money."

"That sounds good."

"It might take a few hours to get it."

Garth was relieved to hear she at least had a plan. "That shouldn't be a problem." Two hours . . . two measly hours and then he could be on his way again.

"What will you do?" Hilary asked politely.

"I'll check with the hotel, but I think our clothes are gone for good. I was thinking maybe I should walk down to one of the department stores and pick out a few pieces of clothing to tide me over."

"Oh . . .that's sounds nice. Would you mind if I tagged along until my money gets here?"

"No, I suppose not," Garth agreed cautiously. He eyed her blanket worriedly. "Just be sure you keep that thing pulled up."

"Maybe I shouldn't go." Hilary quickly reassessed her state of undress. "I might embarrass you . . ."

"I don't see that you have much choice. Besides, if anyone asks why you're wearing the blanket, we'll explain what's happened. Just keep the thing pulled up tight."

Obediently, Hilary hitched the blanket higher. "I will." She smiled up at him through lowered lashes, and Garth felt his pulse quicken.

Don't be getting any ideas about her, he warned himself. *She's nothing but bad news, Redmond. All you have to do is see that she's taken care of for another two hours; then it's So long, sweetheart.*

The reassuring thought made Garth feel better.

* * *

While Garth browsed through the men's department, Hilary phoned her parents in Denver. They quickly assured her they would send the money.

"Hotel fire! Are you sure you're all right? We thought you were going to be staying with Marsha!" Maxie Brookfield exclaimed.

"I'm fine, Mom. Honest. It was so late when I arrived that I thought I'd just stay at a hotel tonight," Hilary fabricated. She hated to mislead her mother, but she didn't want her to know her true predicament. Although Hilary had lived away from home for four years, her parents were still protective enough to worry about her if they thought she was alone in West Creek. Fortunately, Maxie didn't press the issue.

"Honey, don't you worry!" Simon Brookfield's voice came over the line to comfort his daughter. "We'll take care of the problem immediately. You're sure you're all right?"

"I'm fine, Dad. Just wire the money, and I'll pay you back when I get home."

As Hilary replaced the receiver a few minutes later, she thought how nice it was to have parents. Especially understanding ones who asked very few questions.

Tale of Love

Garth was examining a black-and-red flannel shirt when Hilary found him in the men's department.

He thoughtfully eyed his reflection in the full-length mirror, then turned and lifted his brows expectantly. "What do you think?"

"It's nice. You look good in red." *Actually, he would look good in anything,* Hilary found herself thinking. *Or in absolutely nothing . . .* She was shocked to have such thoughts about a complete stranger.

"Did you get through to your parents?"

"Yes. Daddy's making all the arrangements. He'll be calling me back as soon as the transaction is completed. I gave him the number of the store, and the manager said he would be happy to page me when the call comes through."

"Good." Garth said absently. He decided to take the shirt. "We'll just kill time until he calls back."

Glancing at Hilary, Garth felt a tug of compassion. She looked pitiful standing there in that blanket.

"Hey, why don't you pick yourself out a few things? I'll lend you the money, and you can pay me back when your money gets here," Garth offered casually.

105

"Oh, I couldn't. You've been too kind already."

"No, go ahead. You can't run around that way." He was beginning to resent some of the suggestive looks a few of the male shoppers had already given her. "Buy whatever you need."

"It would be so nice . . . if you're sure you wouldn't mind." Hilary jumped at the opportunity to rid herself of the embarrassing blanket.

"I'm sure." Garth disappeared into the dressing room to try on a pair of black trousers while Hilary went off to make her own selections.

She was trying to decide on an inexpensive coat when the saleswoman approached her. "Miss Brookfield?"

"Yes."

"You have a call at the counter."

"Thanks." She grabbed the midcalf-length burgundy coat and added it to the jeans, undies, gloves, and blouse she had already selected. Then she eagerly trailed behind the elderly woman to the service counter.

"Hi, Dad. Is everything taken care of?"

"Honey, now don't worry . . . They're having some sort of a computer malfunction at the Western Union office here, but the money's on its way."

"Good. How long will it take?"

"Well, that's the catch. You won't be able to pick it up until tomorrow morning," Simon explained apologetically.

"Tomorrow morning!" Hilary exclaimed, trying unsuccessfully to hide her disappointment. "Oh, Dad! Can't they get it here sooner than that?"

"I'm afraid not. Just have Marsha drive you to the Western Union office anytime after eight tomorrow morning. The money will be there waiting."

"But Marsha . . ." Hilary caught herself just in time. She realized she couldn't tell him Marsha was in Jamaica, while *she* was stranded in West Creek, penniless, with nowhere to spend the night.

"Hilary? Are you still there?"

"Yes. Tomorrow morning will be fine, Daddy. Thanks. I'll call you and let you know when I get the money," she promised. She quickly hung up before her courage failed.

The saleswoman had overheard the conversation, and Hilary suddenly found herself telling her about her miserable plight. She burst out into a fresh round of tears.

The clerk was just handing her a fresh tissue when Garth approached the counter with his arms loaded with garments.

"What's wrong now?" He dropped the bundle and automatically reached into his back pocket for a handkerchief. He knew Hilary well enough by now to know that she would go through her tissue in a matter of minutes.

Between sobs, Hilary recounted the details of her conversation with her father. At the conclusion of her tearful report, the saleswoman shot Garth an expectant look and leaned across the counter. "The poor little thing is in an awful predicament," she said sympathetically.

"I'm aware of that."

"Good! Then you won't just walk off and leave her?"

Garth eyed the salesclerk coolly. "I hadn't planned on it."

"There, there, dear! I'm sure everything will work out all right." The motherly clerk tried to soothe Hilary. "This gentleman said he would stay with you."

"Oh, thank you, but I've been enough trouble to him as it is." Hilary accepted the handkerchief and blew her nose.

"Let's not panic," Garth said—for the sake

of both women. He reached into his billfold for a credit card. "Put her purchases on here too."

The clerk nodded pleasantly. "If you'd like to slip into the dressing room and put these on, I'll make out the tickets," she told Hilary as she handed her a complete change of clothing.

While Hilary dressed, Garth paid for their purchases, then walked over to the elevator. Leaning down for a drink of water from the fountain, he started and jumped back as the flow spurted up to hit him full in the face. Reaching for his handkerchief, he remembered it was gone.

Sighing, Garth mopped the water off his face with the sleeve of his shirt. He found it hard to believe that just the day before he had been in Chicago—only mildly stressed out.

Hilary came out of the dressing room carrying the neatly folded blanket, her nightie, and her makeup kit. She located Garth and smiled, and he felt his stomach flutter. The jeans and blouse she was wearing fit her like a glove, and he was forced to admit to himself how attractive she was.

"You look better," he complimented her.

He handed her the shopping bag with her other purchases inside.

"Thanks. What's that all over the front of your shirt?" Hilary opened the bag and retrieved the coat and gloves. She slipped them on as he punched the button for the elevator.

"Water."

"Oh." Hilary didn't dare ask him how it got there.

They got on the elevator and rode to the ground floor. As they emerged from the revolving doors a blast of frigid air hit them in the face.

"It's getting colder," Hilary observed.

Pulling up the collar of his new jacket, Garth scanned the sky thoughtfully. "Yeah, it looks like rain."

They paused beside a streetlight, each sneaking an uneasy glance at the other. It would be the opportune time to part company.

"Well . . ."

"Well . . ." The thought of having to spend the night at a bus station or all-night café flashed horrifyingly before Hilary's eyes.

"I suppose we should check with the hotel and see what they suggest," Garth offered.

"Yes, that's a good idea."

They walked back to the Merrymont at a brisk pace, seeking shelter deep in the linings of their coats from the rising wind.

When they arrived it didn't surprise them to learn that the hotel had ceased operations for the time being. There was still a thick plume of black smoke drifting out of the windows of the fourth and fifth floors.

"Well, back to square one," Garth said as they walked back out to the street.

Feeling like an anchor around his neck, Hilary knew the time had come to set him free. He had been nicer than the average person would have been, but she couldn't impose on him any longer. Already she was feeling a dependency on him that she shouldn't feel.

"Garth . . ." He paused and she turned to face him. She had to raise her voice above the rising wind. "You go on. I'll just hang around the lobby of the hotel until tomorrow morning."

"No, I couldn't do that—"

"Yes, you can. I insist. Just leave me your name and where I can return the money you loaned me, and I'll mail you a check when I get back home."

The thought was tempting, and she was making it easy for him. Still, Garth didn't feel

111

he could just walk off and leave her. But Hilary insisted. She made him write down his name and address; then he stepped off the sidewalk to hail a passing cab.

"I promise I'll send the money as soon as I get home," she assured Garth as he hesitantly got into the waiting cab.

"You sure you'll be all right?" Garth felt torn. He didn't want to be responsible for her, yet he found himself reluctant to leave her.

"I'll be fine. Really!"

Garth reached into his back pocket and hastily withdrew his billfold. "Here's seventy-five dollars. See that you get a nice room at one of the other hotels and a good breakfast in the morning." He shoved the money into her hand before she could protest.

"Garth, I couldn't . . ."

Garth slammed the door and rolled down the window. "You can pay me back. Just be careful. There are a lot of weirdos around."

Hilary smiled and clutched the money to her heart. She was suddenly very sad to see her good Samaritan go. "I will. You be careful too."

"I will."

She leaned over impetuously and kissed him. Her mouth felt warm and sweet on his.

Garth closed his eyes, and he felt himself respond to the unexpected reward. The kiss sent a surge of desire through him. He was surprised at his reaction. A simple kiss shouldn't affect him that way.

The embrace was over before Garth knew it, and the cab was pulling away from the curb. He twisted around in the seat, watching as Hilary's now familiar figure grew smaller in the distance.

A feeling of loss came over him as the cab turned the corner and she disappeared from his view.

All the "what ifs?" imaginable flooded his mind as he sank wearily back in the seat. He had a headache; his nose was raw from this miserable cold; and now he felt like a complete ass for deserting her.

Suppose she couldn't find a hotel room? Suppose she ran into that airhead Ricetrum again. Suppose someone tried to pick her up . . . Garth's mind was spinning with all the ugly possibilities. He couldn't be her keeper! He was having a hard enough time coping with his own problems.

But the image of Hilary standing alone on a dark street corner rose up to haunt him. *Damn it, Redmond! You wouldn't leave a dog standing on a corner in this kind of weather, alone, unprotected . . .*

Unable to shake the guilt feelings, Garth suddenly leaned forward and tapped the driver on the shoulder. "Go back to the Merrymont."

"Did you forget something?"

"I guess you could say that." Garth sighed. He had no idea what he was going to do with her. He just knew he couldn't leave her standing on some corner.

As the taxi neared the hotel, Garth shook his head wearily when he saw she was sitting alone on a bus bench, her makeup kit and the shopping bag from the department store propped beside her. The wind was tossing her hair about, and just as he'd suspected, she was crying again.

Garth rolled down his window as the cab eased up to the curb. "Hi, good-looking. You fool around?"

Hilary glanced up, and her eyes brightened. "Only when I'm asked," she sniffed. She tried to make light of her misery, but she had *never* been so glad to see anyone.

"Well, I suppose you could get in, and we could discuss the possibilities," Garth suggested dryly.

He knew he was flirting with her, and for the life of him, he didn't know why.

Hilary grinned and hurriedly reached for the makeup kit and shopping bag before he changed his mind. "I suppose it's worth discussing," she conceded.

After all, she reasoned as she slid in the backseat of the cab next to his comforting warmth, she really didn't have much choice. And she had missed him like the devil the two and a half minutes he had been gone!

Chapter Seven

AS THE TAXI PULLED BACK INTO the line of traffic, Hilary jerked her gloves off with her teeth and unbuttoned her coat. "Where're we going?"

"Beats me. You got any suggestions?"

"Sorry, I ran dry several calamities ago," Hilary confessed. "Listen, I really appreciate your coming back for me."

"I thought you were going to get a hotel room," Garth reminded.

"I was . . . but I didn't know where to begin looking." Hilary's face suddenly broke out
in a relieved grin. "Honestly, who would ever
think two people could run into so many ob-
stacles just trying to spend a quiet vacation?"

Garth was busy looking out of the window
for a hotel or motel with a vacancy sign. He
was barely listening to her prattle. "Yeah, who
would ever think," he answered absentmindedly.

Hilary edged forward on the seat and
peered at him intently. "You're doing okay,
aren't you? I mean, all this hasn't been too
much for you, has it?" If the poor man had
been under stress before, Hilary knew the last
few hours couldn't have helped.

"No, I'm fine. How about you?"

She sighed. "I'm adjusting."

"Where to, buddy?" The cabbie peered in
his rearview mirror, waiting for directions.

"To tell you the truth, I don't know," Garth
confessed. "Would you have any idea where
we can get a room for the night?"

"Around here?"

No, in Honolulu! Garth thought irritably.
"Yeah, around here."

"For the entire night?" The driver sneaked
another peek in the mirror and noted that

neither one of them had luggage. They were both carrying shopping bags from Garfield's. It must be whoopee time again.

"There's a meat-packers' convention over at the Bellview and a pharmaceutical convention over at the Bell Tower." The cabbie took off his hat and scratched his head. "What with the Merrymont fire, I think just about everything in town's full up this evening." The cab turned the corner and shot down Gamin Boulevard. " 'Course, I know a little place over on Fairfax that rents out rooms for a couple of hours or so . . ."

Garth felt his face turning a bright red at the cabbie's mistaken interpretation of his request. "Uh, no, we need something for the night," he mumbled.

The cabbie's mouth turned up at the corners in a tiny smirk. "Well, like I said, that's gonna be tough."

"Ask him if he knows someone who would just rent us a room for a little while," Hilary whispered.

Garth's gaze slid up guiltily to meet the cabbie's in the rearview mirror. "Are you serious?" he snapped out of the corner of his mouth. "He already thinks the worst."

"But if there's no hotel or motel vacancies,

maybe there's a boarding house around that would be willing to rent us a room." Hilary realized it was a long shot, but at this point she was ready to concede they were desperate.

Seeing the immediate color flood Garth's face again, she added, "I wouldn't mind sleeping on the floor . . . if you'll just spend the night with me."

"Uh . . . Hilary . . ." Garth knew the driver was listening to their conversation.

The cabbie grinned as he reached into his shirt pocket for a cigarette.

"No, really! I'll do anything you say if you'll just stay with me tonight, Garth."

While sitting on the lonely bus bench, Hilary discovered she'd lost whatever self-confidence she thought she'd possessed. She wasn't beyond begging Garth to stay with her. It hadn't taken but a few minutes to realize just how disconcerting it was to be completely alone in a strange town. Hilary would gladly sacrifice her pride if he would promise not to leave her alone again.

"I'll even pay you"—Hilary upped the ante hopefully—"as soon as I get my money."

Lucky devil! the cabbie thought enviously.

Garth's face turned several shades of red as he diverted his attention to staring out of the window again. "Why don't we stop at a restaurant and have a cup of coffee? We need to discuss this in private." Garth was determined to avoid the cabbie's widening smirk in the rearview mirror.

"Oh . . . Well, sure," Hilary agreed, wondering why both men suddenly had such strange looks on their faces. "You won't try to get away from me again, will you?"

"No . . . and I didn't try to get away from you earlier," Garth said quietly. He wished she would change the subject.

Hilary leaned back in the seat and let out a sigh of relief. "Good. I'd hate to have to call Daddy again."

Garth leaned forward and spoke curtly to the cabbie. "She means she had to call her father for money and . . ." He broke off lamely, realizing he could never explain the confusing situation. "Just pull over at the first restaurant."

"Whatever you say, Romeo!"

The taxi screeched to a halt a few minutes later in front of Red's Sirloin Parlor. Garth paid the amused driver as Hilary got out of the cab. He noticed she was limping again.

"How's the ankle?" he asked as he held the door open for her to enter the restaurant.

"I think it's getting worse."

"It looks as if it's swelling more."

That didn't surprise her. It was throbbing to beat the band.

"You get us a table, and I'll grab a newspaper."

Garth spotted the vending machines at the corner. As crazy as it sounded, Hilary's earlier suggestion of a boarding house might be their only chance to avoid sleeping on a park bench tonight.

While Garth went for the paper, Hilary asked for a table for two, and was promptly seated. As she sank into the comfortable red leather seat, exhaustion overcame her again. She realized she couldn't take much more of this merry-go-round. She was tired and grimy, and she longed for a hot tub where she could soak her ankle and a soft bed on which to rest. Was it only hours ago that she had experienced all those wonderful luxuries she had always taken for granted?

Hilary absently picked up one of the bread sticks the restaurant had provided and bit into it. Her eyes widened as she crunched down on something grainy.

Removing the foreign object from her mouth, she was dismayed to find it was a small piece of enamel from a tooth. She deposited what she had chewed in a napkin, and with her tongue she probed the jagged edge of a molar. She groaned out loud.

This had been the worst day of her life!

When Garth returned with the papers Hilary told him about the latest catastrophe, and he shook his head compassionately.

"I ordered coffee," she told him as he unfolded the paper and began scanning the classified ads.

"Good." He handed her a section of the ads. "Here, see what you can find."

"Okay."

"By the way, what time is it?"

Hilary glanced at her watch. "Eight-thirty."

"Brother!"

"What's wrong?"

"Nothing. I was just thinking that it's getting late to go looking for a room at a boarding house."

"Yes, I know."

The waitress brought their coffee and set it down before them. "Anything else I can get you?"

Hilary smiled. "No, thanks . . . unless you can recommend a good eye doctor, an ankle doctor, a dentist, and a place to stay the night."

The waitress walked away, smiling as if she thought Hilary was kidding. Hilary wished she had been.

"She didn't believe me."

"Who in their right mind would?"

They sipped their coffee and browsed through the ads, reading one out loud every few minutes.

"Here . . ." Hilary leaned forward and pointed to an ad in the third column. "This sounds like a nice one."

"I should hope to shout it does!" Garth protested. "Look at the price."

"Oh, yes. Sorry." She was leaning so close that he could detect a faint whiff of her perfume. For some crazy reason Garth suddenly felt himself becoming aroused.

Now that was *all* he needed to make his day, he thought irritably. He folded the paper shut.

"You keep looking. I'll call and check on a couple of these." He slid out of the booth and walked to the pay phone.

Hilary picked up her coffee cup and studied him from under lowered lashes. She was enjoying his company. He was wearing a nice, clean-smelling aftershave . . . intriguing and sensuous. She took another sip of coffee. It seemed to her he got better-looking by the minute. Not pretty-boy handsome, but his face had enough interesting planes and angles to make a woman look twice.

Hilary wondered how many women there were in Garth Redmond's life, and she was surprised to feel an unreasonable twinge of jealousy at the thought. She barely knew him; yet she found herself feeling almost possessive.

Garth returned to the table in a few minutes, waving a piece of paper at her triumphantly. "These two are still available."

"Wonderful! Can we look at them right away?"

"I told them we'd be there within the hour."

The taxi pulled up in front of the first house, and Hilary looked at Garth and smiled. "It looks lovely."

"Right now, I'd settle for a pup tent," Garth confessed.

The landlady greeted them at the door with a warm and friendly hello. "My name is Mrs. Biggerton, but you can call me Mary," she said.

Hilary and Garth nodded and smiled politely.

"Mr. Biggerton always said our guests should call us John and Mary—God rest his soul." Mary dabbed at the corners of her eyes. "John was such a good man."

Lamely, Hilary and Garth nodded again.

"The room . . . ?" Garth prompted.

"Oh, yes, the room. Just follow me, dearies."

My, my, Mary thought. *What a lovely couple they make.* She was reminded of herself and her late husband. She and John had been just about this young couple's age when they had bought this old house. *How grand first love is!* she thought as she led them up the carpeted stairway.

"It's a lovely, lovely room. Nice big windows facing the south. Very quiet. Old Mr. Whitlock has the adjoining room, but he doesn't give anyone a minute's trouble," Mary promised as she unlocked the door and motioned them into the room.

Garth saw all he needed to make a quick decision. The room had a bed, and it appeared to be clean. He turned to Hilary who quickly gave her approval with a hasty nod.

"It looks good to me," she agreed.

"Good. We'll take it."

"Oh, my!" The landlady smiled at them benevolently. "I was hoping you would say that. Now if you and the missus will follow me, we'll take care of the registration."

Garth was about to clarify the *missus*, when he saw Hilary's warning look.

They walked back down the stairway, listening to Mary chat about her pet canary, Wiladeen, who was feeling under the weather. "I'm afraid she's caught a draft, poor thing. And with the weather predicted to turn so bad . . . well . . . I only hope Dr. Saddler can drop by before too much longer."

Garth glanced at Hilary. He wondered if a draft could be fatal to a canary.

Hilary lifted her shoulder bitterly. If it were *her* canary, it would be.

As they entered the front hallway, Mary glanced out of the picture window and noticed that the taxi was still waiting at the curb. "Oh, dear! If you'd like to get your luggage, I'll wait here for you," she offered. The cab's meter was running, and the poor little things were probably having to watch every penny, Mary reasoned. She felt sorry for young people today. Everything was so expensive.

Hilary appreciated Mary's concern but

quickly pointed out, "We don't have any luggage . . ."

She realized immediately that she'd said the wrong thing.

A giant iceberg suddenly floated into Mary's eyes. "You don't have any luggage?" she asked.

"No . . . You see, we actually need the room for just one night . . . because all the hotels are full . . ." Hilary's voice trailed off lamely as the iceberg suddenly grew in size.

"One night?"

"Yes, you see—"

"Why, the two of you should be ashamed of yourselves!" Mary marched over to the door and yanked it open self-righteously. "Go! Out of here with you! I run a decent, God-fearing establishment, and I don't hold with none of this kinky one-night stuff."

"Excuse me, Mary, but we're not—" Garth started to protest, but Mary cut him off abruptly.

"*Mrs.* Biggerton to you! Why, John would roll over in his grave if he thought I was party to such goings-on. The very nerve!" Mary stuck her nose in the air. "Out!"

"But, Mary . . ." Hilary tried to explain again, embarrassed by the woman's mistaken impression. "You see . . . no, we aren't married, but we were staying at the Merrymont and—"

"Oh, *please,* young lady! Spare me the details!" Mary pressed a hand over her thundering heart. "Mind you now, I'm not one to moralize, but you two should be ashamed of yourselves. Your parents certainly would be!"

"You don't understand . . ."

But Hilary's attempted explanation was ignored as Mary pivoted on one foot and stalked away. "I'll have no part of this! No, sir, not in this house! And I'll thank you to show yourselves out!" Mary was still ranting about "today's decadent society" as she disappeared through the kitchen doorway.

Hilary turned to confront a red-faced Garth. "You devil, you! Are you trying to corrupt me?" she deadpanned.

Garth sighed as he ran one hand through his hair. "I have the distinct feeling the room isn't available anymore."

"Strange, I have that same feeling."

They quietly let themselves out the front door.

"I don't know what you're laughing about," Garth admonished as they got back into the cab. "It's close to ten o'clock, and we still don't have a place to spend the night."

"I know." Hilary settled herself in the back-seat and picked up the classified ads again. "But we will," she predicted optimistically.

At the next stop they were admitted inside the house by a big burly man who constantly winked at Hilary whenever Garth's head was turned. Recalling the bad impression they'd made on Mary Biggerton, Hilary cringed to think how this insinuating clod would miscon-strue the situation.

Hilary heard Garth's quick intake of breath as the man unlocked the door to the apart-ment and let it swing open.

The small room was appalling. Beer cans were strewn across the coffee table, and there were several bags of trash standing in the middle of the kitchen floor. Just how long they'd been there, only heaven knew. If the sight hadn't nauseated Hilary, the smell cer-tainly did.

She tried not to breathe as she trailed closely behind Garth. She hoped he was as horrified as she was, yet she was resolved to yield to his decision. Whatever he decided, she would have to accept.

Glancing at the soiled spread that was

draped haphazardly across the sagging bed, Hilary reminded herself that she really wasn't *that* tired. She could sit up in a chair all night and let *him* have the bed.

Garth continued to pretend polite interest in the room. True, they were desperate, but nobody could be *this* desperate, he thought glumly. He was surprised that the man had the nerve to show the apartment without first having bulldozed the place out.

"It's a little messy," the landlord granted. "The ol' lady don't get off work till eleven, but if you want the room, I'll send her up as soon as she gets home. She can spruce it up a little." He ripped the tab off a beer can and took a long swallow as his eyes ran over Hilary suggestively. "Won't take long, once she gets her butt in gear."

Hilary clamped her hand over Garth's arm and began to squeeze tightly.

Garth glanced at her questioningly.

"My foot. . ." Hilary shuddered as a large brown roach scurried across her shoe and disappeared under the bed.

"Damn bugs! The exterminator was here last week, and the little varmints have been runnin' wild ever since." The landlord set his beer can down, jerked the metal bed away from the corner, and proceeded to stomp the offending creature into a greasy pulp.

So much for available room number two.

"Well, now what?"

In the taxi once more, Hilary sucked in the welcome fresh air and tried to forget the unspeakable carnage they had just witnessed.

Garth struggled to make a decision he'd avoided all evening. It looked as if he'd be forced to make it now.

"My grandparents have a beach house," he finally admitted.

Hilary glanced at him in disbelief. "Here . . . in West Creek?"

"Yes . . . but I didn't want to go there until tomorrow night."

"Why not?"

"My cousin Dorothy, her husband Frank, and the most obnoxious kids I've ever encountered—that's why not," Garth confessed. "But even *they* are beginning to sound good."

"Are they staying at the cottage?"

"Yes, but they're supposed to leave tomorrow night. As much as I hate to admit it, I don't think we have any choice but to join them."

"I can stand it if you can," Hilary assured him.

Garth wasn't sure he could, but he figured his options had just run out.

The taxi eased to a stop in front of the cottage on Oceanside Drive. The weathered bungalow was surrounded by neatly manicured hedges. Garth paid the driver, grabbed the two Garfield shopping bags, and escorted Hilary up the sidewalk.

"What are we going to tell your cousin?" Hilary fretted. She could imagine how Dorothy would view her staying with Garth.

"I don't know about you, but I'm telling them good night. Then I'm going straight to bed."

"Not me. I'm heading straight for a hot bath."

"I don't see Frank's station wagon around anywhere. They must be out sightseeing." Garth reached under the mat to retrieve the extra key.

"I feel terrible just barging in like this."

"Wait until you meet Frank and Dorothy. You'll get over it."

"Garth!" Hilary frowned, and he grinned.

They stepped through the doorway, and Garth flipped on the lights. Setting the shopping bags on the small love seat, he walked into the living room, switching on lamps as he went. Hilary followed closely behind as her eyes appreciatively scanned the homey cottage.

"This is really nice," she said gratefully.

"Yeah, I always thought so. It has all of Gram's personal touches." Garth's smile was affectionate as he pointed toward the multicolored afghan that was draped across the back of the sofa.

"Did she do these?" Hilary was closely examining the finely detailed cross-stitched pictures that adorned the south wall.

"Yeah, those too. Wait until you see the kitchen—if the kids have left it standing. Grandpa is a carpenter by trade, or at least he was until he retired. He did all the cabinetwork."

Hilary followed him into the kitchen, and Garth switched on the lights.

If the living room echoed Garth's grandmother's creativity, the kitchen proved that his grandfather was equally talented. "My goodness, this is lovely!"

"You really like it?"

Hilary walked over to the cabinets and ran her hand over the polished oak admiringly.

"This is exactly the sort of cabinet I'd like in my own home someday."

Garth smiled and thought of how Lisa would hate the cabinets. They wouldn't be modern enough for her. "Grandpa always says when I get married he'll build me a house."

Hilary's gaze met his shyly. "And are you planning on getting married soon?"

"No . . . not soon. How about you?" Garth regretted mentioning the subject as he saw the sadness come into her eyes. "Sorry, I didn't mean to remind you of Lenny."

"That's all right. Lenny and I never discussed marriage," she admitted.

"I date a woman who'd like to discuss it, but I'm not ready yet," Garth said.

"Oh."

Glancing at the kitchen table, Garth noticed a note propped against the ceramic salt shaker. He picked it up and read it, then released an audible sigh of relief. "Looks like we may have gotten our first piece of good luck."

Hilary glanced at her watch. "Let's note the hour, for posterity's sake," she joked.

"Looks like Frank decided to leave a day early so he could rest up before going back to the office."

"Oh. Well, at least that will make it easier for you." Hilary pulled a chair away from the kitchen table and sank onto it gratefully. She began absentmindedly rubbing her swollen ankle.

"That ankle still bothering you?"

"A little."

Garth knelt down and took her foot in his hand. The ankle was red and swollen to twice its normal size.

"Sit right there, and I'll have you fixed up in no time," he promised.

He rummaged beneath the kitchen sink and produced a small porcelain pan. He put the tea kettle on the burner to heat water, then poured a small amount into the pan a few minutes later. After adding cold water, he tested the temperature, then carefully slipped her shoe and ankle hose off and lowered her foot into the basin.

"How's that?"

"Fine." Actually, Hilary thought it was pretty close to heaven.

While she soaked her ankle, Garth rummaged through the pantry and retrieved a small first-aid kit. "Gram's always prepared," he explained as he opened the lid and reached for the Ace bandage. "When you're through, I'll wrap it for you."

While Hilary indulged herself, Garth made them each a cup of tea, and they lapsed into an easy, relaxed conversation.

"So you're a flight controller," Hilary mused aloud. "That must be very interesting."

"Yes, I've always liked my job, but it can get hectic at times."

"Tell me something—how in the world do you keep all those planes from running into one another?" Hilary asked.

Garth laughed. "Well, I don't. At least, I'm not responsible for *all* of them. Let's see, how can I explain it simply? The east-bound flights fly at odd altitudes—twenty-seven hundred, twenty-nine hundred, or thirty-one hundred feet, etcetera. West-bound flights fly at even altitudes."

"But doesn't that bring them dangerously close to one another?"

"No, not at all. They're separated by distances of a thousand feet vertically, and ten miles laterally."

"Then you agree that flying is the safest way to go?"

"The safest way *to go?*" Garth grinned. "We

try to avoid that phrase, but yes, I believe the skies are safer than they've ever been, despite what you hear to the contrary. Between 1981 and 1985, the airlines flew one billion passengers through twenty-six million takeoffs and landings, with an average fatality rate of ninety per year. Compare that to the hundred and twenty-three people killed daily in car accidents—that's an average of forty-five thousand deaths a year. And flying is even safer than walking, which takes seven thousand lives a year."

"I don't mind the flying. It's the circling—when my plane hasn't been cleared to land—that makes me nervous," Hilary confessed.

"It shouldn't worry you. It's just a normal holding pattern when traffic's stacked up. The planes are still separated by a thousand feet, and they're being closely monitored on radar. When a plane at the bottom of the stack is cleared to approach and land, then the others are individually and systematically instructed to descend a thousand feet."

"Simple," Hilary jested.

"At times," he agreed.

It was nice to talk to each other. Hilary and Garth's moods were less pessimistic by the time Hilary had removed her foot from the basin a half hour later. She surveyed the foot and grinned. "It's beginning to shrivel." She gingerly lifted the waterlogged foot, and Garth reached for the towel. "I'll get that for you," he said.

"You don't have to. I can . . ." Hilary began to protest. She suddenly felt extremely shy. She reached for the towel, knocking it from his hand.

Bending to retrieve the linen, they found their faces inches apart. The unexpected closeness caught them both by surprise.

"I can do that," she said softly.

"I'd like to do it for you."

Hilary had a fluttery feeling in the pit of her stomach. Garth's look was warm and suggestively intense.

As if a magnet were drawing them together, their mouths slowly moved toward each other. They touched.

His lips were sweet and inviting as they lingered on hers, caressing and light. Hilary closed her eyes and felt the room begin to tilt crazily. She held her breath, hoping he would take her in his arms and deepen the kiss. But as suddenly as it had begun, the embrace ended.

Garth cleared his throat and handed the

towel to her. "Maybe you're right. You dry the foot, and I'll wrap it."

Hilary touched her tongue to her lips. She could still taste his presence. "All right."

When the ankle was properly wrapped, Garth suggested they go straight to bed. "There's only one bedroom, so I'll take the sofa," he offered.

"Please, take the bed. I don't mind sleeping on the sofa."

"The sofa will be fine. I'm so tense I'll have to take a sleeping pill to relax. Believe me . . . I'll be out in five minutes," Garth assured her.

Rummaging through the shopping bags, Garth found the package of T-shirts he'd purchased earlier. "You can sleep in one of these."

"Thanks. Would you care if I took a bath first?"

Visions of Hilary naked, soaking in a hot tub, rose up to tantalize Garth.

"No. Make yourself at home. There's a bathroom second door to the right. I'll use the one off the utility room."

"Thanks. Well, I guess I'll see you first thing in the morning."

"Yeah . . ." Garth's eyes moved over her

lazily. "If you're up first, Gram keeps the coffee in the refrigerator."

"How do you like your eggs?"

Garth's eyes unwillingly dropped to the gentle swell of her breasts, and he was mortified to hear *his* voice saying, "Fried . . . with double yolks."

Chapter Eight

HILARY AND GARTH SAID GOOD night, and Hilary walked down the hall to Garth's grandparents' bedroom. She was still smiling.

The way Garth had looked at her a few minutes ago and the crazy way her pulse had jumped when his gaze slid admiringly over her breasts . . . Well, maybe Lenny wasn't going to be as hard to forget as she'd first thought.

Hilary opened the door and switched on

the lamp beside the bed. The small bedroom emerged in a warm light. The furnishings were homey and comfortable, and the full-sized brass bed beckoned invitingly.

In minutes Hilary had slipped out of her blouse and jeans and had drawn a tub of hot water in the adjoining bath. Instead of a leisurely soak, however, she found she wanted to wash as quickly as possible and get into bed.

At Garth's suggestion, she availed herself of Grace Redmond's liberal assortment of creams and lotions sitting on the vanity. Then she slipped into the T-shirt he'd handed her earlier.

The garment totally engulfed her petite frame, and Hilary found herself running her fingers sensually over the soft material, thinking about its owner.

Hilary knew Garth had never worn the shirt, yet she found herself visualizing how the material would lie against the broad expanse of his chest . . . the way it would mold and cling to all those muscles . . . With that tantalizing thought, she felt the beginnings of desire. It was strange. She would ordinarily be thinking about Lenny; yet now it was Garth—

a man she had known for such a short time—who suddenly dominated her fantasies.

She pulled back the fluffy comforter on the bed and climbed between the crisp sheets. The mattress welcomed her tired body with a cushioning embrace. Outside, a shutter banged against the side of the cottage, and Hilary could hear the breakers rolling in from the Atlantic.

It seemed as if the wind had been picking up steadily all evening. Hilary hoped it wouldn't interfere with plane departures the following morning. She planned to go to Western Union and collect her money, then call the airport and book a flight to Denver. Soon this whole crazy escapade would be a memory . . . with the exception of Garth. Hilary had a feeling he was going to linger in her mind a good deal longer.

She lay in the dark, going over the past few hectic hours with a surprising fondness. How unexpectedly they'd come into each other's life.

Had his pulse raced as erratically as hers did when they touched? Snuggling more deeply within the folds of the comforter, Hilary warned herself that she was becoming much too attached to Garth Redmond.

For all she knew, he could be in love with the "Lisa" he had mentioned earlier . . . And there was Lenny to contend with . . . And Hilary didn't know a thing about Garth, other than the fact he was attractive . . . kind . . . understanding . . . incredibly gentle.

The memory of his unexpected kiss set off a series of flutters in the bottom of her stomach as she eventually drifted off to sleep.

Garth had to manhandle the stubborn sofa cushions. He unfolded the thin foam mattress from the metal cage of the sofa, then rummaged for ten minutes before he found an extra blanket and pillow in the hall closet.

As he passed Hilary's room, he wondered if she was asleep. He had heard her moving about earlier, but all was quiet now.

Running his tongue over his lips, he could still taste the faint traces of her lipstick. Why was it that one kiss had aroused him so swiftly, so unexpectedly, so fully that he had had to fight the urge to make a pass at her? Crazy, that's what it was. The woman was not only dangerous to his libido but together they made a dangerous couple. It was as if a curse were on both of them, yet Garth found Hilary increasingly appealing.

Slipping off his shoes, he climbed into bed, then tried to remove his pants beneath the sheet. Snagging his sore toe in the metal frame of the sleeper, he bit his lower lip to stifle an agonizing moan.

Damn! Might as well try sleeping on a bed of nails!

The thin slice of foam rubber, which some-one had mistakenly labeled a mattress, had a tendency to curl up slightly at either end; and the metal support bar across the middle seemed determined to become embedded in the base of his spine.

Rolling back out onto the floor, Garth reached for his trousers and withdrew the small packet a doctor had given him a few months ago when he'd complained of a succession of sleepless nights. The strong medication was to be taken only when necessary, but Garth knew, at the rate he was going, he had to have it now.

He walked into the kitchen, drew a glass of water, and popped one of the pills in his mouth. A few moments later he was back in bed, trying to find a safe harbor away from the tormenting support bar.

As the sleeping pill began to take effect, Garth's eyelids drooped heavily. Hilary's image floated temptingly before him. Hilary . . . sleeping in the next room, in his shirt . . . unrestricted . . . unencompassed . . . eggs . . .

Garth groaned and rolled onto his stomach. He slammed the pillow over his head to block out the sound of the wind and his confused thoughts.

Sometime around three in the morning, Garth flipped over on his back. He could hear the wind howling outside the beach house.

Ordinarily he was a light sleeper; but under the influence of the medication, he found it nearly impossible to open his eyes. Trying to fight off the effects of the sleeping pill, Garth finally managed to sit upright in bed.

He shook his head in an effort to clear his vision. His eyes narrowed as he focused on the large protuberance at the bottom of his bed. Groping at the bulge in the blankets, he jumped when he heard a feminine voice respond in a sleepy voice.

Sometime during the night, Hilary had crawled into bed with him. She recoiled when a hand touched her bare bottom.

"What in the . . . Hilary, is that you?" Garth leaned over and heatedly addressed the bulge.

"Yes" came the muffled reply.

"What are you doing?"

"Trying to sleep."

"In *my* bed?"

"Yes."

Garth sighed and ran his hand through his tousled hair. "You want to come out of there?"

It was hard enough for Garth to ignore his growing attraction to her. Now she was in his bed . . .

There was a slight pause; then Hilary slowly emerged from beneath the blanket. She was embarrassed he'd caught her, but she quickly decided that the sense of security she'd felt while snuggled safely under the covers was worth the sacrifice. It had been either join Garth in his bed, or continue to lie petrified in her own while her mind amplified the sound of the wind as it slapped angrily at the beach house.

Hilary crept out of the sheets, up the long, muscular length of his body, and settled easily on his chest. It was much wider than she had first estimated. He was bare-chested and undeniably gorgeous. Hilary wasn't usually so audacious; yet she felt completely at ease lying on top of him.

Garth's eyes met hers distraughtly. *"Now* what are you doing?" The feel of her lying pressed tightly against his bare chest sent his hormones on a rampage.

"The wind is blowing," Hilary explained lamely, realizing that he was probably going to demand that she go back to her own room.

"So?" His voice was still thick with sleep.

"So . . . I was frightened . . ." Her fingers slipped through the thick mat of hair on his chest and lingered there.

"Frightened? Why were you . . . Stop that!" Garth removed her hands, but she quickly wrapped her arms around him and buried her face in his neck.

"Please, I've always been terrified of the wind," Hilary pleaded. "Just let me stay here with you for a while."

Garth tried to shift her, aware that she was going to be shocked if she moved in the wrong direction.

"Look"—he eased her to his side, settling her in his arms as he would a small child—"there's nothing to be afraid of. It's just a little wind."

"I was in a tornado once," she confessed,

trying to offer him some sort of explanation for her radical change in behavior. "I was terrified."

Garth felt a shudder ripple through her, and he pulled her closer. "Okay, if it makes you feel any better, you can stay with me for a while." He was too tired to think straight, and she was doing crazy things to his libido. But it was a mistake to let her stay, and he knew it.

Hilary sighed, and her arms tightened around his neck appreciatively. "Thank you."

Garth lay back on the pillow and closed his eyes for a moment. He felt fuzzy and light-headed from the medication. He drifted off for a moment, thinking about Hilary in his arms. He desired her. Wouldn't any man in his right mind? But he wasn't thinking clearly. They'd known each other only a few hours, and Garth wasn't about to jump into what could easily become a sticky situation.

But she felt incredibly good in his arms. Soft and tiny like a kitten . . . and she smelled so feminine. The tantalizing scent drifted over Garth . . . Her bare legs were next to his, and they felt as smooth as silk next to his hair-roughened ones.

Garth stirred restlessly. "Hilary . . . about you and Lenny Ricetrum—"

"Please, I don't want to talk about Lenny."

"Are you sure? You've been pretty upset about him." Garth absentmindedly began to caress the outline of her bare thigh. Maybe if he reminded her of Lenny she'd realize that they were putting themselves in a dangerous position, lying this close . . .

"Lenny seems like a million years ago," Hilary confessed as she snuggled more deeply into his arms. It wasn't Lenny who was upsetting her. It was Garth. Hilary was afraid he would realize what his hand was doing—and stop.

But his hand continued to meander slowly up the silken length of her. Supple fingers paused once or twice to massage the small of her back.

Hilary, secure in the realization that he *did* realize what he was doing, began to relax.

"You shouldn't do that," she protested half-heartedly when he touched pleasure points, causing a quickening of her pulse. She hated herself because she couldn't manage to sound more convincing.

"Just relax," he murmured smoothly, and his hand continued its alluring path up her spine, sensuously kneading and exploring her satiny skin. Even in his sluggish state, Garth knew he should stop. But he couldn't—even if he'd wanted to. Wasn't she openly inviting him to take advantage of the situation? Together in the same bed, she was clinging to him as if they were already lovers.

His mouth lowered slowly to search for hers, and a thrill shot through him when he found hers eagerly waiting.

They kissed, their soft murmurs of pleasure blending as his hand moved under the T-shirt to her bare breasts.

The kiss deepened, and Hilary felt herself go limp in his arms as the gusts shook the house with growing ferocity.

She realized that what she was doing was rash and totally out of character, yet she was returning his kiss with a reckless abandon, pressing ever closer . . . encouraging his advances . . . almost begging for them.

Had the past few hours indeed pushed her over the brink to insanity?

Garth shifted his weight, and his kisses became more ardent as he pressed her back against the pillows.

"Garth . . ." Hilary murmured as their mouths parted a few moments later. He nibbled warm kisses down the column of her neck. "Is there another woman . . . ?"

"Another woman?"

"Is there someone special in your life?" Hilary hesitated to ask, but the answer could make a difference.

"No." Garth started to kiss her again, and then he paused. Lisa seemed so distant since he'd left Chicago. Almost as if she no longer existed in his life. "No, that's not quite true." He amended what he'd said. "I've been seeing a woman for the past few months, but we're not engaged."

"Do you plan to marry her?"

"No." The finality of his answer surprised him. A heavy weight felt as if it had suddenly been lifted off his shoulders. "No, I don't," Garth repeated again more firmly. "I just realized that."

"What we're doing is reckless," Hilary warned, teasing his mouth with the tip of her tongue. "We barely know each other."

"I know."

"I don't make a habit of this."

"That's nice to know." He rolled over with her in his arms and began to slide the T-shirt up over her head.

"Garth." Hilary's eyes met his, and he saw confusion clouding the pools of glistening blue sapphires. "I don't want you to think I'm easy." She had gone mad. There was no longer any doubt in Hilary's mind.

"I don't think that." He kissed the tip of her nose, then took her mouth again as his fingers began to arouse her with an expertise that left her breathless. Garth was careful to keep his own desire in check as their passions began to soar. Hilary heard his suppressed moan, and her own spiraling needs urged him on.

Garth murmured her name urgently as the storm continued to build.

Hilary was suddenly seized with panic. What was she doing in his arms, about to let him make love to her? She didn't know a thing about him. It seemed imperative that they know *something* about each other!

"How many children are there in your family?"

"What?"

"Children . . . do you have any brothers and sisters?"

"Two younger brothers."

"I have an older sister. What's your favorite dessert?"

"Cheesecake."

"I favor lemon pie."

"That's nice." Garth's mouth took hers fiercely.

"School?"

"What?"

"Where did you go to school?"

"In Chicago . . . Why?"

"Are you a college graduate?"

"Yes . . . Are you?"

"Yes." They rolled over, and Garth lay on top of her now.

"What about your grades?"

"They were okay . . . I made the Dean's honor roll."

Hilary felt her heart sink. She'd been lucky to eke out passing grades.

"What kind of a car do you drive?"

"Damn it, Hilary! Do we have to discuss this right now?"

"No, I just thought we should know something about each other."

"I know I'm going crazy," Garth whispered. "Let's talk later."

Hilary decided she'd found out all she needed to know.

In his arms she found a joy, an awareness she had never known before. he was gentle yet firm, demanding yet giving, eager to have her experience the ultimate fulfillment along with him. She knew she was falling in love and was powerless to stop it.

Garth suddenly groaned as he lost control. He joined her in completion, and they soared and spiraled in the climax of their loving. Tears rolled unabashedly down Hilary's cheeks at the beauty of the moment.

"What's the matter?" Garth whispered once the tides of passion had crested explosively, then slowly began to ebb.

"It was so . . . perfect."

He smiled and wiped the wetness off her cheeks with his thumbs. "It isn't anything to cry about."

"I cry when I'm happy."

"And when you're sad . . . and when you're hungry . . . and when you're—"

Hilary tenderly covered his mouth with her hand. "True. I'm a mess."

"No, you're beautiful," Garth corrected her. Hilary was sure she saw something very close to love in his eyes. "And you've made me very happy." Their mouths met again affectionately.

"The wind is getting worse," Hilary murmured a few moments later as Garth settled her in the crook of his arm.

"If it'll make you feel better, I'll take a look outside," Garth offered sleepily. "Those old shutters have always been loose, and when they rattle it makes the wind sound worse than it really is."

"I would feel better . . . but be careful."

"I planned on it." Garth slid out of bed and immediately stubbed his sore toe on the metal leg of the bed. He hopped painfully on one foot as Hilary wadded the corner of the sheet in her mouth to keep from laughing.

He looked at her incredulously. "You think this is funny?"

Hilary quickly sobered up. She shook her head, no.

Garth stepped into his pants and yanked the zipper closed. "I'm going to lose that toe if I hit it one more time!" he grumbled.

Hilary agreed and stuffed the sheet in her mouth again, her eyes crinkling with suppressed laughter.

Garth reached over to tickle her ribs, and she collapsed on the pillow. They wrestled on the unsteady frame for a few minutes before it threatened to collapse. He finally kissed her again and got up. His head spun like a top, and he groped for support.

"Damn! I should never have taken that sleeping pill."

"How strong was it?"

"Enough to knock a bull moose out cold for twenty-four hours."

Hilary grinned. "Go check the shutters; then we'll both try and get some sleep."

"Believe me, Ms. Brookfield, there are very few women I would go out at this hour to check a shutter for," Garth complained.

He slipped his jacket on and opened the front door. The sudden impact of the violent wind threatened to knock him off his feet. "Holy . . ." he exclaimed. It was pitch-black, but from where Garth stood he could see that the trees lining the cobblestone walk were practically bent over double in their surrender to the strong gales. In the distance he could hear the roar of the breakers rolling in from the ocean.

"What's the matter?" Hilary was waiting just inside the door.

"The wind . . . It's going crazy."

"I told you so."

"Those breakers have to be at least four feet high," he exclaimed.

"Is it a hurricane?"

"I don't know. Stay where you are." Garth shut the door, and Hilary crept back into the warmth of the bed.

She plumped the pillow, keeping one ear

tuned to the wind as she thought about the way Garth had made love to her. Was it possible that only a few hours ago she was crying over a lost love, and now she could barely remember what Lenny looked like?

Was it possible to fall in love with a man so totally, so completely, in such a short span of time? Or was it merely the strange set of circumstances she and Garth found themselves in that caused the strong attraction? Hilary wasn't sure.

Intimacy was an act she'd never taken lightly. She viewed sex as a serious commitment, but she didn't know how Garth felt about the subject. Hilary rolled over and stared at the front door. Where was he? He'd been gone only for a few minutes, she reminded herself. He couldn't possibly have had time to fix the shutters . . . But then it was so dark and windy out there. What if something had happened to him? Panic seized her as she hurriedly slipped out of bed. Wrapping herself in the blanket, she hobbled to the door and pulled it open.

Oh, my gosh! She held her breath in awe. She had never seen such violent winds. "What is it?" Hilary had to shout to make herself heard.

Garth was busy trying to secure one of the flapping shutters. "What?" He cupped a hand to his ear questioningly.

"I said is it a hurricane?" Hilary shouted.

"Hurricane?"

She nodded.

"I don't think so. I think the season's over." Garth leapt back up on the porch as an icy rain started to plummet down from the overcast sky.

Hilary went in search of a towel as he shrugged out of his wet jacket. Moments later she returned and handed him the towel.

"If it isn't a hurricane, what is it?"

"I have no idea. I suppose it could be a hurricane, but they're usually over by mid-November." Garth vigorously rubbed his hair dry with the towel. "But by the looks of things, I'd say we're in for something more than a typical winter storm."

"With the way our luck's been running, I'd have to agree."

Garth glanced up and grinned. "Let's see . . . What could be worse than a hurricane?" he prompted.

"Typhoon?"

"I doubt it. We're on the Atlantic side."

161

"Not for long," Hilary predicted. "Not the way that wind is blowing."

Garth pitched the towel on a chair and walked into the kitchen to switch on the radio. He scanned the range of the dial but couldn't find a weather report. He set the dial on an easy-listening station, realizing that most stations have periodic weather announcements.

Hilary kept glancing out of the window and pacing back and forth across the floor nervously. Garth was still trying to fight off the effect of the sleeping pill, so he wandered back into the living room and draped himself across the sofa.

"Are you going to sleep—in this storm?" Hilary asked.

"No." Garth yawned. "I'm just resting my eyes." His voice trailed off sleepily as he began to get warm.

Hilary shook her head in disbelief, then went into the kitchen to get closer to the radio.

Garth nodded off briefly, only to be awakened a few minutes later by Hilary tapping on his shoulder.

"Huh?" He tried to force his heavy lids to open.

"What's a 'ziggy'?"

"A what?"

"A *ziggy*."

"Some sort of a model . . . I think." Both eyes drooped shut again.

Hilary shook his shoulder. "No, that was Twiggy! What's a *ziggy*?"

"Damned if I know." Garth tried to cover his ears with a pillow, but Hilary blocked the effort.

"Listen, Garth. There's something really strange going on. Wake up!" She reached over and turned up the volume of the small radio she had brought in from the kitchen.

". . . We interrupt this broadcast again for an updated report on the winter-storm watch. The National Weather Service has issued a severe winter-storm warning for the entire coastal region. Winds gusting up to fifty miles per hour, unusually high tides, and surging waves are expected. The National Weather Service has urged residents to complete all safety precautions and evacuate to higher ground inland as soon as possible."

Hilary listened wide-eyed as the weather forecaster continued his gloomy report.

"The severe coastal storm is being attributed to the nearly straight-line configuration of the earth, sun, and moon. It is estimated that this alignment takes place once in every eighteen and a half years. *Syzygy* is the technical term for this celestial lineup, which occurs when the moon is aligned directly opposite the earth and sun, or between the two bodies. Both sun and moon are far south of the equator; and the moon is at perigee—its closest approach to the earth in a month. Either alignment causes a bulging of the tides in some areas of the earth. Keep tuned for updated reports—"

Having heard all he needed to for the time being, Garth reached over and switched off the radio.

"What are you doing?"

"Eighteen and a half years! And the syzygy picks this time to show up again!" Garth smacked his pillow angrily.

Hilary watched as he slowly rolled to his feet, trying to focus his vision.

"Where are you going?"

"Apparently this thing is going to get a whole lot worse before it gets any better. We've got work to do."

"Don't you think we should leave?" Hilary

trailed helplessly along behind him as he went in search of a rain slicker.

"And how do you suggest we do that—call a taxi?" He asked dryly.

"We could try."

"Check the phones. I'm betting most of the lines are down in this area."

When Hilary picked up the receiver, she was met with an ominous silence. Her face grew pale. "What will we do?"

Garth paused and pulled her up to his chest. He tipped her face up to give her a brief, reassuring kiss. "I'm sorry. I know you're scared, and I have to admit I'm a little concerned myself. But we'll be fine."

"I'm frightened."

"After what we've been through? Living through a little 'ziggy' should be a breeze!" He made light of their predicament.

"Are you going out again?"

"Yes. We can't just sit here. My grandparents keep a good supply of plywood out in the garage. They've lived through a few coastal storms in their time." Garth smiled encouragingly. "Quite worrying."

"Oh, Garth! This is all my fault."

"Why?"

"I saw that 'ziggy' word mentioned in the newspaper, but I didn't bother to read what it meant."

"It's *syzygy*." Garth pronounced the word *SIZ-uh-jee*. "And don't feel guilty. I'm the one who's at fault. I knew about the storm watch for this area, but as of yesterday the forecasters hadn't been able to predict how serious it would be. Besides, I was so preoccupied with my own problems that I didn't pay much attention."

Hilary appreciated Garth's attempts to minimize her fear. "Do you really think we'll be safe here?"

Garth nodded. "I'd better get at it, though. I've got a lot of nails to drive."

"I'll help."

"What about your ankle?"

"It's fine." Hilary forced herself not to limp as she turned toward the bedroom to get dressed.

Garth caught her arm to detain her. "Hey, lady"—he pulled her back into his embrace and kissed her again with incredible tenderness—"you're okay, you know that?" he asked when their lips finally parted.

"Thank you. I've been hoping you'd notice." They kissed once more; then he swatted her bottom playfully and sent her on to get dressed.

Nailing the bulky sheets of plywood over the windows was a slow, tedious process. Especially when one of the carpenters was trying to fight off the sluggish aftermath of a sleeping pill, and the other one was trying to keep her weight off the sprained ankle she kept forgetting about.

Despite deep yawns and countless ouches, the work was eventually completed.

Around midnight the tired twosome stood back to assess their work. Garth watched Hilary's eyes as they reflected pride in their accomplishment.

She'd sure proved to be made of stronger stuff than he would have expected from the weeping, helpless girl he'd encountered twenty-four hours ago. If she hadn't held the awkward sheets of plywood, Garth would still be struggling to nail them to the window frames. She'd taken time out to brew a pot of strong coffee, and they had drunk several cups as they continued to work.

"I wish we'd had enough plywood to cover the garage windows," Hilary brooded.

"They'll be easy enough to replace."

With the work completed, Garth changed

his mind about staying through the brunt of the storm. "Maybe we should try to get to higher ground, now that the house is secured."

"All right. But first"—Hilary pointed to a faint light in the distance—"we need to see if those people need our help."

Garth glanced at the cottage occupied year-round by the Johnsons. They were near his grandparents' age; and the last time Garth had seen Ben, arthritis had taken its toll on the aging man's hands.

The self-designated rescue team hurriedly headed into the wind and crossed the yard.

Ben and Esther Johnson welcomed the offer of assistance. Hilary and Garth pitched in and worked throughout the night, praying that their efforts would save the cottage from complete destruction.

"Don't you think we should try to get to higher ground, Ben?" Garth asked as the last of the windows was sealed off.

"Nope. Me and Esther's been through some pretty rough times. We'll be staying."

Garth glanced at Hilary, who smiled. The strain of the past few hours was evident on her pretty features. "We'll be staying with you —if you don't mind," Garth said.

"Nope. Welcome the company."

The brunt of the storm was predicted to hit around three that morning. Ben, Esther, Hilary, and Garth sat huddled in the Johnsons' living room to wait out the raging winter storm. Around two o'clock, Esther and Ben nodded off to sleep.

"Are you doing okay?" Garth whispered as he cradled Hilary in his arms. They were sitting on the sofa, listening to the rain pounding on the weathered roof.

"I'm fine. Just a little tired." Hilary yawned as she rested her head on Garth's shoulder. She was exhausted, but she had never been happier. "How's your cold?"

"I hadn't thought much about it. I guess it's better."

"Good. You tired?"

"Yeah, bushed." Garth sighed as he stretched long legs out in front of him and rested his head against hers.

"Garth . . . about what happened earlier."

Garth didn't answer for a moment. Somehow he sensed she wanted to talk about the intimacy they'd shared, but he wasn't sure he did. He needed time to sort through his mixed feelings. Though he couldn't explain it, he knew Hilary had touched a portion of his heart that no other woman had ever touched before. Finally, he responded to her prompting. "What about it?" he asked softly.

Hilary moved her head until it rested comfortably on his chest. Her finger toyed lightly with the button on his shirt. "I'll never forget tonight . . . or you."

Garth stroked her hair affectionately. "I won't forget either." She felt so small and helpless in his arms . . . so *right!*

"Will you call me occasionally?"

Garth chuckled. "What do you want me to call you?"

Hilary sighed. "Darling . . . sweetheart . . . honey . . ."

He sighed and buried his face in her hair. He wasn't sure if she was teasing or not.

Hilary laughed, and she could tell he was considerably relieved. "Just call to say hello once in a while. Let me know how you are . . . where you are . . ."

Hilary couldn't imagine not ever seeing him again, but she knew it was entirely possible, once they went their separate ways.

"Sure. Why not? And you can give me a ring every now and then."

She decided to pay him back for his earlier jibe. "What sort of ring do you want?"

"Is this where I'm supposed to say 'a wedding ring'?" Garth asked calmly.

Hilary raised her face to meet his, her heart suddenly in her eyes. "Of course, not . . . Unless you want to."

Garth chuckled at her candor and kissed her deeply, drawing a response from deep within.

When their lips parted many long moments later, he promised softly, "I'll think of you often."

"Make sure that you do!" Hilary wanted more—much more. But it was a start.

"I'm hungry."

"Me too." Their mouths touched, lingered, reluctant to part.

"We'll eat a steak ten inches thick when this is all over," he promised, trailing a finger through a damp strand of her hair.

"You'll have to buy it for me," she reminded him.

"I'll buy you the moon if you want it." His mouth closed hungrily over hers again, sealing the promise with another long kiss.

Exhausted from the hard work and the all-night exposure to cold winds, they settled down in each other's arms and dozed, secure in the knowledge that, at least for the moment, they still had each other.

Chapter Nine

THE WINTER STORM RAGED FOR hours. Fierce winds pounded at the thin sheets of plywood nailed to the windows, and cold rain poured from repeated cloudbursts, promising the aftermath of severe flooding.

It seemed Mother Nature was intent upon showing the true force of the power she held over the elements. Even the salty sea responded to her show of uncompromising strength as it hurled its brutal waves against the deserted shoreline.

Hilary lay listening to the wind. Her stomach rolled turbulently as she thought of being devoured by the angry ocean. The only thing that kept her from succumbing to her terror was the comfort of Garth's arms. With him by her side, she felt she could endure anything.

The storm continued for what seemed like endless hours before it finally began to abate. With dawn came the calming of the ruthless winds, although the rising sun was still obscured behind a thick mass of clouds.

"It looks like it's about over." Ben stood at the front door of the cottage and viewed the aftermath of destruction, thankful that the cottage had survived another onslaught.

Garth stirred on the sofa and gently nudged Hilary. "Come on sleepyhead. We need to check on Gram's cottage."

"Is it finally over?" Hilary sat up self-consciously, trying to arrange her tousled hair into some semblance of order.

"It's still raining, but the winds are beginning to let up." Garth was anxious to view the storm's damage.

Hilary and Garth stepped out onto the porch a few minutes later. The ravaged remains that greeted them were distressing.

Trees were down, their sharp, splintery

ends a mere mockery of the splendid strength they had once possessed. The front lawn of the cottage had been turned into a small lake.

Garth and Hilary descended the steps to wade ankle-deep in icy water. It was no longer pouring, just an icy drizzle fell from the clouds.

"Your cold, Garth . . . It will get worse," Hilary fretted as they sloshed their way across the yard.

Garth sneezed and pulled the slicker up closer to his face. "Watch where you're going. There's a lot of debris."

Shattered pieces of wood drifted past, fragments of small abandoned boats that had fallen prey to the pulverizing winds. In the distance they could see a deserted beach house bobbing, roofless, in the turgid waters. The structure had been too weak to withstand the main onslaught of the storm.

Garth threaded his way along the beach while Hilary followed, clinging to his jacket for stability.

"And what, fair lady, should we do on this third day of our lovely vacation?" Garth joked as he stopped long enough to sneeze a couple of times into his handkerchief. "I'm sick of all this relaxation! Let's do something exciting!"

Going along with his sudden spurt of joviality, Hilary pretended to give the matter serious thought. "Oh, dear, I don't know. There's so much we haven't done, yet. Earthquakes, locust plagues, aviational disasters—"

"Oh, sorry. I almost covered that one on my flight to Raleigh, but everything turned out all right at the last minute."

"Honestly?"

"Honestly. The landing gear malfunctioned on my plane," Garth admitted.

"Well, I suppose that makes up for the blowout my cab had on the way to Stapleton . . . and for my sprained ankle."

"Yeah, I suppose that makes us even-up on good times."

They looked at each other and grinned. "At least *you* aren't half blind," Hilary said accusingly. "I lost my contact at the airport."

"I know. I stepped on it."

Her mouth dropped open. "You *what!*"

"I can see . . ."—Garth ignored her astonishment and went on listing his miseries—"I just can't breathe because of the pneumonia I got when my cab was stuck in traffic, and I was forced to run the rest of the way to O'Hare."

By now, each of them was striving hard to keep a straight face.

"You had plenty of time to buy cold pills during the layover in Raleigh," she said reproachfully.

"No, I spent those particular eight hours handing out clean handkerchiefs to some strange—and I do mean strange—woman who was crying every time I looked up."

"How sad!" Hilary's grin widened. "You didn't have cold pills in your luggage?"

"I didn't *have* luggage by that time."

"But you could have purchased some when you arrived at your hotel."

"Oh, by then I had my luggage back," he conceded.

"You did?"

"Yes, only the hotel burned down, and I lost it again."

They lost their composure at the same time and began laughing over their ridiculous string of bad luck. Hilary sagged weakly against him, and he almost went down in the water.

"You should have seen your face when Lenny grabbed you around the throat!"

Garth steadied himself and looked at her incredulously, shocked that she would have

177

the gall to mention the humiliating incident. Hilary dissolved in a new round of merriment.

"You thought that was funny? You're sick! That baboon could have broken my neck!"

Hilary nodded sympathetically. "I know!"

She dissolved in laughter again, but Garth shook his head in disgust. He hadn't found Lenny Ricetrum all that amusing.

When Hilary's giddiness had finally passed, Garth reached over and pulled her to him for an overdue good-morning kiss.

"Hell of a vacation, Ms. Brookfield, but you've definitely made it worthwhile," he said a few moments later.

"Thank you, Mr. Richmond. We must do it again sometime."

As they neared the Redmond cottage, they were relieved to see that it was still standing. Garth didn't even mind that its shingles were all curled or that the windows of the garage had been blown out during the night. As they drew nearer, the waters were beginning to recede.

"My feet are like blocks of ice," Hilary complained. She huddled more deeply into the lining of her jacket.

"Mine too." Garth sneezed again.

Until last night his cold had seemed to be getting better. This morning there was a tightness in his chest, and the cold water he was standing in set him shivering with a renewed chill.

Garth reached over and took Hilary's hand as they walked around the corner of the garage. "I want a hot cup of coffee and some dry clothing."

The sight of Lenny Ricetrum sitting on the front porch was the last thing Garth had expected. Hilary stopped abruptly when she saw him. She tugged warningly on Garth's jacket as he trudged on toward the porch, ignoring the unwelcomed visitor.

"Uh-oh . . . Look who's here."

"I noticed, but *he* can move on this time."

"But, Garth . . ."

Garth ignored her protests, and they continued walking toward the cottage. Personally he planned to ignore the two hundred and twenty pounds of foreboding flesh sitting on the doorstep.

Lenny stood up and crossed his arms. His look openly dared them to try and walk past him.

Garth had just about had it. What was supposed to have been a relaxing vacation had turned into a nightmare of unbelievable proportions. From the very start of this bizarre journey two days ago—*just two days ago*, Garth thought despairingly—he'd run into one disaster after another. Now, to add to his problems, he'd become intimate with Hilary Brookfield, who just happened to have an ex-boyfriend who was big enough to hunt bear with a switch.

What had he done to deserve this?

The sight of the baboon who had earlier tried to twist his neck off, who was now trying to block the entrance to *his* home, kindled a spark of anger in Garth.

"How did you find us, Lenny?" Hilary demanded as they approached the porch.

"Let's just say I'm not as dumb as you think I am."

"I didn't say I thought you were dumb. I just thought I had made it clear that I was going to need a little time to think about our situation—"

"Can it, Hilary!" Lenny interrupted curtly. "This is between me and ol' lover boy right now."

"My name is not *lover boy*, Ricetrum, and I don't appreciate your talking to Hilary in that tone of voice," Garth warned. His brown eyes sparkled with a stubbornness Hilary had never seen there before.

"Lenny, I want you to leave." Hilary hurriedly stepped between the two men. She was afraid Lenny would actually hurt Garth this time.

Garth calmly set her aside.

"But, Garth!"

"I can take care of this, Hilary."

"Hilary, I told you to can it!" Lenny snapped.

"And I told you, I don't want you talking to Hilary like that." Garth stepped forward, meeting Lenny's cold stare with one equally glacial.

"Oh, yeah? How would you like me to talk to you—with these!" Lenny doubled up his two beefy fists and shook them threateningly at Garth.

Garth stiffened with resentment. "Be my guest!"

Hilary clamped her hand over her mouth as Lenny suddenly sprang from the porch like a panther.

The force of a man twice his weight slamming into him so abruptly promptly knocked Garth back flat on his back. Lenny gripped

Garth's head, landing a brutal punch to the right eye. It split the skin wide open on impact. Blinded by mud and blood, Garth struggled to deliver his own blows.

Hilary stood paralyzed with fear, watching the unfairly matched pair as they rolled around in the mud. The tumbling finally halted with Lenny sitting straddled across Garth's chest.

"Come on, Ricetrum! Can't we discuss this like two adults—" Garth's plea was cut off as another meaty fist slammed into his mouth. He swore and rolled his head to one side to spit blood.

The two began frantically wallowing around again at Hilary's feet. She realized she'd have to do something—and fast.

The sight of blood oozing from the cuts on Garth's face gave her the strength she needed. She crouched aggressively as her temper surfaced in full force.

"Lenny, you get off him this instant!" Like a mean banty rooster, Hilary flew between the two struggling men.

In her eagerness to assist Garth, she slipped and fell facedown in the mud. She paused only long enough to rake away the gook from her eyes. Crawling the rest of the way on her hands and knees, she pounced on Lenny's back.

"What are you doing?" Lenny tried to shake the unexpected wildcat off his back. But Hilary's fingers grabbed a hank of his black hair and jerked painfully. Lenny let out a yell, and the momentary distraction afforded Garth a well-targeted right to Lenny's face.

As Lenny's hands shot up to protect his nose, Garth was busy trying to free himself. Lenny's fruitless efforts to sling Hilary off his back left her head spinning long after his attempts had slowed down.

"I said let him go, Lenny!" Hilary enunciated in an ominous voice just before she yanked hard on his hair again.

"*Ouch!* All right, all right! Damn it, Hilary! Let go of my hair!"

Finally giving up on his hoped-for reconciliation, Lenny lifted himself from Garth, whose face was completely covered with mud.

Lenny made a feeble attempt to straighten his dishevelled clothing. He could take a hint. It was obvious that Hilary was no longer interested in him.

Reaching up to rub his smarting head, Lenny gave it one more try. "I'm warning you, Hilary. I'm flying back to Denver in an hour, and if you don't come with me right now I'm washing my hands of you—permanently."

Hilary rose to her feet unsteadily, her clothing covered with thick mud. "Well, happy trails to you!"

Lenny shot her a dirty look and stalked off angrily to his rented car. Moments later he wheeled out of sight.

Garth sat up and stared at the muddy woman who had come to his rescue. Even with her hair dripping filth, Hilary was nothing short of beautiful as she hovered over him and offered her hand in assistance.

Garth lifted one brow wryly. "Happy trails to you?"

Hilary shrugged. "I couldn't think of anything better."

Though he realized he would have a shiner later on, Garth couldn't remember when his spirits had been higher. Hilary had flatly refused to go back with the jerk.

Hilary put a protective arm around Garth and helped him carefully to his feet. "We'd better get you into some dry clothes."

"*We?*" Garth grinned.

"You're sure a frisky little devil—right after

the tar's been beaten out of you!" Hilary chided. She decided to ignore his suggestive tone. "Lean on me."

"I didn't get the tar beaten out of me," Garth protested. "Ricetrum's going to have a black eye too." He draped his arm around her neck and nuzzled her ear playfully. "Um . . . you taste like mud!"

Hilary avoided his amorous advances and pointed him in the direction of the cottage. "Let's get you into the shower and rinse off some of this mud before it sets like cement."

"Will you get in with me?"

She blushed. "You're getting awfully bold."

"It's our vacation! We should have a little fun," Garth complained. He felt good. She'd actually refused to go back with Ricetrum!

While Hilary adjusted the water temperature in the shower, Garth examined his injuries in the mirror. He decided he hadn't come out all that badly. He could've been dead!

He licked the salty blood off his split lower lip and frowned. "Why couldn't you have been dating a hundred-pound weakling?"

Hilary grinned. "You did okay."

"I did, didn't I? Did you see that right punch I threw at him?"

"I saw. It was impressive. Come over here."

Garth obeyed and she helped him—clothes and all—into the shower. When he was safely in the stall she started to close the door, but he reached out and grabbed her hand.

"Now, stop—"

"Get in with me."

"No!"

"Yes! You know something?" His eyes met hers, and Hilary felt she could see right into his soul. And it looked as if he had feelings that he couldn't comprehend himself.

"No, what?" She knew she shouldn't take the bait, but she did anyway.

"For a minute I was afraid you would go back with Ricetrum," he confessed.

"Would that have bothered you?"

He smiled back at her. "Yes . . . I think it would have."

Hilary felt the return of butterflies in her stomach. "I'm glad. Lenny Ricetrum is history, as far as I'm concerned. I'm not sure what I ever saw in him."

"I'm not either. I didn't think he was your type," Garth admitted as he pulled her into the shower with him. He wrapped his arms around her waist possessively. "Kiss me."

Hilary didn't wait to be invited twice. She

moved into his waiting arms, and they exchanged a long, satisfying kiss.

"Are you hungry?" he murmured sexily against her lips.

"Ravenous!"

"Me too!"

They both knew they weren't talking about food.

With a control that had his insides trembling, Garth's hand captured her chin and his thumb gently caressed her lips. "Thank you."

"For what?"

"For standing up for me against Lenny."

Hilary could feel the sweet pulse of desire coursing through her as he began to peel away her muddy clothing. "I can't explain how I felt when I saw you were in danger . . ."

"Try!" Garth urged as he quickly stripped out of his clothing, then pulled her close so that her bare body was pressed against his.

"I was frightened . . . I was so afraid Lenny would hurt you . . . and I didn't know what I would do if he did." Hilary's words dissolved as she felt the touch of his lips on her breast.

"You're beautiful," he whispered as the tip of his tongue moved with unbearable lightness across her skin. Waves of pleasure surged through her as he continued the sensuous assault. "And desirable . . . exciting . . ."

Hilary curled her fingers into the thick mass of his hair, pressing her body against his solid, comforting length. Nibbling lightly at the lobe of his ear, she added one other description, which only served to send a hot shaft of desire ricocheting through him.

"And very wicked!" Garth scolded.

"That wasn't wicked."

"Who told you it wasn't?" His mouth caught hers demandingly.

After a long, arousing kiss Garth whispered his own observation, and she laughed softly.

"You're terrible!"

Garth chuckled and gave her a big bear hug. "You know what?"

"No, what?"

"This has been a terrible vacation, but I can't remember ever feeling as good as I do right now."

Hilary laughed, sharing his jubilant mood. She was happy, but she had to remind herself to keep the whirlwind relationship in perspective. The feelings were still too new for her to hope they could ever last.

As the hot-water heater's supply began to

run out, Garth lifted her into his arms and stepped out of the shower.

"Garth . . . we shouldn't," Hilary warned. Barely controlled passion was clearly evident in his eyes now.

"Why not?"

"Well, last night . . . was last night. When you go back to Chicago, and I return to Denver . . ." Her voice trailed off lamely. Her body throbbed with longing; she wanted him as badly as he wanted her.

He looked into her face, full of defenseless love, and assured her gently, "I can't imagine ever forgetting you."

He moved to the brass bed and laid her down tenderly. Then his hands were in her hair, drawing her closer and stilling her murmured protests with the perfect union of their mouths. Soft rays of sunlight filtered through the sheer material of the drapes as he sought to weaken her resistance as surely as she was weakening his.

He brought her body flush against him, proving his need for her. A tender light shone in his eyes as he whispered in a voice made more urgent with desire. "If it's the short period of time we've known each other that bothers you, then I won't make love to you again," he promised. "But I'm afraid you'll have to be the one to make that decision."

"Until I met you, I would have never dreamed I could be so reckless," Hilary confessed.

"Reckless? I don't think what we have is reckless."

"It is for me, Garth. I want permanence in life . . . and I think it's too soon for us to commit ourselves to such a relationship. We barely know each other."

"No, not yet. But in time . . ." Garth lowered his mouth to take hers. The rational words lingered, but the desires of the flesh were more persuasive.

Lavishing her throat with feather kisses, he warned again. "Say the word and I'll stop."

Hilary thought he wasn't being fair. Her hazy mind didn't have the slightest idea of what "the word" would be.

"I don't want you to stop," she confessed and drew a shuddering breath. He was kissing her with a seductive torment that was more eloquent than words.

"Maybe there isn't any word that could stop me," he conceded. His mouth moved down the perfumed length of her, touching her here . . . and there . . . and there . . .

Maybe nothing could stop him from claiming her again, Garth realized.

Maybe this crazy roller coaster he had been on would turn out to be the real thing.

Maybe . . . He would think about it later.

Chapter Ten

HILARY WAS THE FIRST TO awaken. Her hand moved to caress the warm form lying next to her. When it came in contact with a masculine, hair-roughened thigh, she smiled. She hadn't been dreaming. Garth had made love to her again—no, it had been more than making love. Something wonderful and exciting had taken place last night, and she was sure he'd felt it too.

She sighed and rolled toward him as his arms drew her tightly against his bare length.

He was still asleep, and he looked so peaceful that she was sure there was still a special warmth that lingered from their spent passion.

The little clock sitting on the nightstand drew her attention. She gasped softly when she realized they'd slept for a straight fourteen hours!

Turning back to Garth, she teasingly traced the dark circle under his left eye, Lenny's legacy.

Black eye or not, he was the most handsome man in the world, she thought wistfully. More importantly, he was a good man . . . perfect husband material. Hilary sensed he would be wonderful with children, and she'd bet her last dollar he would even love his mother-in-law. He just seemed to be the type.

Propping herself up on her elbows, she tenderly brushed her lips across his bare shoulder. "Mrs. Garth Redmond. Hilary Redmond. Garth and Hilary Redmond," whispered, liking the sound of all three.

Garth moved and his eyes opened slowly. Hilary smiled and kissed the tip of his nose affectionately.

"What are you doing?"

Sorry that she'd disturbed him, mostly because she'd been caught, Hilary said guiltily, "Tasting."

"Tasting?"

"Yeah." She poked the tip of her tongue in the crease of one of his dimples and licked him playfully.

"What do I taste like?" he mumbled.

"Um . . . like . . . gentleness, passion, kindness—things like that." Her mouth found his, and they kissed a long, leisurely good morning kiss.

When their lips parted, Garth gazed into her eyes lovingly. "I didn't know you could taste things like gentleness and kindness."

"Not all men taste like that." She absent-mindedly traced his lower lip with the tip of her finger. "But you do, Garth."

"You give me too much credit."

"No, I don't. You're wonderful."

Garth was embarrassed by her praise, but he loved it. "You think so? Come here." He pulled her on top of his chest and kissed her again. "Let's see what you taste like."

Hilary closed her eyes and savored the butterfly kisses that he sprinkled across her forehead, her nose, finally coming to rest against the fullness of her lips, his tongue gently probing the warm moistness of her mouth.

195

"So . . . what do I taste like?"

Garth gazed into her passion-laden eyes and said softly, "Let's see." He paused, gliding his tongue back across her lips, tasting, sampling her sweetness. "I think you taste like . . . gentleness, kindness, and passion."

"But I don't have all those qualities. I anger too easily; I have no patience at times; and while I'm not a mean person, I'm not necessarily overly kind." She hated to admit it, but it was all true.

"What about passion?"

"Well now, passion is possible," she confessed humbly.

"Possible!" Garth lifted a dark brow dubiously, and she grinned.

"Well, maybe probable," she amended, vividly recalling the night before.

"I should think so!"

"Want me to prove it?"

"I thought you'd never ask!"

Entwined in the warm embrace of each other's arms, they gently rolled over, and Garth hungrily captured her mouth again. As their insatiable need for each other flared up again, Garth buried his face in the full softness of her hair and confessed she actually tasted sweet—very sweet. For the next thirty minutes they made love with such ardor that it left them both spent.

With passion temporarily appeased again, Hilary lay quietly in his arms. Garth wondered why she'd suddenly grown so still. He glanced down and nudged her gently. "Hey, sleepyhead, don't drift off on me. It's getting late."

"Um . . . just a few minutes . . . two winks at the most," she pleaded.

Garth glanced at the clock and was astounded to see the time. "Not a chance! I'm starving. Let's forget breakfast and find ourselves a nice thick steak."

The thought of food enticed Hilary to move ever so slightly beneath the sheet. Prying one eye open, she bargained, "And a hot, fat, baked potato—drenched in butter and sour cream?"

Garth nodded sleepily.

"Salad, rolls, and lemon pie?"

"Cheesecake."

"Both!"

"Good Lord!" He smacked her on her bare fanny and rolled out of bed. "How do you keep your figure, eating like that?"

"I just don't worry about it. I usually eat

anything I want and suffer terrible guilt later."

Garth chuckled, recalling how Lisa forever counted calories and became outraged when he refused to do the same. "I'll buy you anything you want. Let's just get a move on."

"All right, but I get the shower first." She playfully tossed her pillow at him as she sprang to her feet and headed toward the bathroom.

Intercepting the flying pillow with one hand, Garth sat up in the bed and watched as she disappeared through the doorway. "Want some help?"

"No. Not if you want to get to the restaurant anytime in the near future," she called back.

Garth rolled out of bed and went over to the door. He rapped loudly. He could hear the sound of water running, so he knew she would be standing beneath the warm spray now.

He remembered all too well how beautiful she looked with her silky skin glistening, the gleaming beads of water sliding down the length of her supple frame . . .

"Just a shower—I promise I won't start anything," he pleaded as he pressed his face against the closed door.

Hilary laughed and shouted above the stream of hot water, "Not a chance. You could be lying."

"No, I promise."

"I thought you were hungry!"

There was a meaningful pause. Then, "I am."

At the suggestive innuendo in his voice, Hilary felt herself weakening. The hot-water heater did tend to empty its supply rapidly—and he did have that miserable cold . . . She tried desperately to rationalize what she was about to do.

"Please!"

With a resigned sigh, she stepped out of the shower and unlocked the door.

"I knew you'd break down." Garth grinned and reached for her slippery body as she tumbled willingly into his arms.

"I told you I was weak."

"I remembered." Garth ran his hands exquisitely over her bottom while he kissed her, then let them drop back to his sides repentantly. "Okay, I promised. But may I at least soap your back?"

"Only if you'll shampoo my hair too," she

bartered as she stepped back in the shower and turned to face the spray of warm water.

"I don't know how to shampoo your hair," he protested.

"You shampoo yours, don't you?"

"I don't think it will be the same."

By the time Garth had lathered her hair, Hilary looked like a creature from outer space.

"Garth! You've used too much shampoo," she complained, spitting the soap bubbles out of her mouth.

He was unconcerned. He was too busy sculpting various animal shapes out of the white froth.

"And here is an attack zebra!" he announced, scooping up a handful of the soap suds and backing her into the corner of the shower.

"Garth, no!" She dodged as he—and the attack zebra—masterminded an offensive on her body that eventually ended with another round of lovemaking.

Later, while she dried her hair, Garth dressed and headed for the Johnsons' cottage to call a taxi.

The level of the small lake in the front yard had descended more rapidly than he'd expected. He was glad its icy waters no longer sloshed over the tops of Silas's old rubber boots.

It was more than two hours before the cab arrived.

As they settled themselves in the backseat, it occurred to Hilary that she hadn't phoned her parents as she'd promised. She'd even forgotten to pick up the money they'd wired her.

"Garth, before we find a place to eat, could we stop by the Western Union office and pick up my money? I was supposed to have picked it up hours ago. My parents are probably sick with worry."

"Of course. I had forgotten all about the money. I suppose we'd better stop by the Merrymont and file an insurance claim while we're at it."

"I suppose so." Hilary snuggled closer to him.

"After we've had dinner." Garth leaned over and nibbled on her ear.

"By all means. Let's eat first."

By the looks of things, the small town of West Creek was still in a state of emergency. Utility workmen were busy repairing fallen power lines, and merchants were removing the bulky sheets of plywood that had saved their plate-glass windows. In the lower-lying areas, families could be seen sweeping the icy waters out of their flooded homes.

Hilary's money was waiting when they arrived at the Western Union office. She signed the required forms, collected her funds, then phoned her parents in Denver.

"Daddy?" Hilary began hesitantly. She wasn't sure if her parents knew of the storm.

"Hilary! What on earth happened to you? We heard on the news about a storm back there, and we were worried sick when we didn't hear from you!" The sharp tone of her father's normally mild voice assured her they knew the full extent of the damage caused by the syzygy.

"Daddy, I'm fine," Hilary said soothingly. She glanced at Garth and made a patient face. "The storm wasn't as bad as the news media made it sound."

Garth grinned, realizing she was trying to downplay the extent of the nightmare they had just weathered.

"When you didn't call us back, naturally we assumed the worst. Your mother's been having fits!"

"I'm sorry, Daddy. Lines are down, and I

wasn't near a phone that worked. Tell Mama I'm fine. Really!"

"I will, baby. Is Marsha all right?"

Hilary looked at Garth and smiled. "She's fine, Daddy. Couldn't be better."

"Are you going to cut your vacation short because of the storm?"

"I think so. I'll let you know what I decide."

When Hilary said good-bye and hung up the phone, Garth looked at her tenderly. "That was nice of you."

Lisa would have played the crisis to the hilt; yet Hilary had went out of her way to spare her parents' feelings. Garth admired her more every hour.

"What was nice?"

"The way you deliberately spared them extra worry."

"Why should I worry them? The storm's over, and I'm still in one piece."

"It was still nice of you." Garth leaned over and kissed her.

"Well . . ."Hilary wrinkled her nose at him lovingly. "I've had a good example to live by lately."

The taxi left the Western Union office and drove to the restaurant. Fortunately for their growling stomachs, the Steak House had escaped severe damage.

Garth eyed the broken neon sign outside the restaurant. "How do you want your *teak?*" he teased, making playful reference to the *S* that had been sucked away by the strong winds.

Hilary smiled, thinking how nice it was to be able to enjoy life again.

Garth escorted her from the taxi and offered her his arm. Hilary graciously accepted it, and with a look of pride etched on his face, he guided her into the restaurant.

"How's the ankle feeling?" He had almost forgotten about her injury.

"What ankle?" she grinned. "How's the cold?"

"What cold?" Garth bantered. The words were barely past his lips when another sneeze hit him.

In no time the hostess had them seated and served. Hilary couldn't remember when a baked potato had ever tasted so good. Garth remarked that his steak was prepared exactly the way he liked it, and he savored every bite with exaggerated pleasure.

Over coffee and cheesecake, the lightness

of their mood slowly shifted, becoming more serious.

Garth reached over and picked up her hand, then kissed the back of it gently. "I'm glad we've had this time together."

Hilary sensed that the hour she'd been dreading had finally arrived. For a second she considered confessing that she had fallen in love with him. But at the last moment she changed her mind. She wasn't sure he was ready to hear that yet. He had never talked of the future.

"I'm glad we have too, Garth."

"The past few days have made me think about a lot of things . . ." His words faded as he groped for a way to express his feelings. He wasn't exactly sure what they were himself. She'd just come out of a bad relationship, and it was too soon for her to start a new one. As for him, he certainly didn't want to jump into anything he couldn't get out of later if he wanted to.

Hilary absentmindedly toyed with her coffee cup, keeping her gaze from his. She wanted desperately to tell him how she felt, but she was afraid. If she expressed her love, and he didn't share the feeling . . .

"Hilary, I guess what I'm trying to say

is . . ." Garth paused, poking his fork at the half-eaten cheesecake.

"Garth, you don't have to say anything," Hilary told him. She didn't want to hear the dreaded "It's been nice, but see you later, kid" routine. She'd rather part with the fragile hope that what they'd had was real. Maybe with a little time, Garth would realize it too.

"Hilary . . . I need a little time—"

"Garth"—she reached over and covered his hand with hers—"you don't have to explain. I know." He was struggling with his doubts, and she wasn't going to push.

"I'll call you . . . And you stay in touch with me." Garth troubled eyes searched hers for an answer she didn't have. "Okay?"

Hilary sighed. At least he wasn't shutting the door entirely. It was more than she'd expected but achingly less than she wanted.

"Okay."

Garth felt a sinking sensation in the pit of his stomach. Had he hoped she might argue with him? "Okay, we agree to keep in touch?"

"Yes, of course." Hilary squeezed his hand reassuringly.

His gaze grew incredibly tender, and he held on to her hand tightly. "You're one hell of a woman."

"Thank you." Her own eyes glistened brightly with unshed tears. "You're quite a man."

Forcing a front of bravery, Hilary quietly excused herself and left for the sanctuary of the ladies' room before the telltale tears could slip down her cheeks. Once she was safely behind closed doors, she gave into the heartfelt sobs. She would never see him again, she agonized. He would go back to Chicago and forget that Hilary Brookfield had ever existed.

Torn between an aching heart, which told her to stay and try to change his mind, and a rational mind, which cautioned her to leave before she got in any more deeply, Hilary reluctantly admitted to herself what she had to do.

She'd go back to Denver first thing in the morning. Maybe getting back to a normal routine would help her get her life in order.

When Hilary returned to the table, she was dry-eyed and wearing a bright smile. Over second cups of coffee, she told Garth of her plans to leave for Denver on the early-morning flight, reasoning that she really should be getting back to the office. "I left on such short notice, and with Marsha gone . . ." Hilary shrugged. "I think I've had all the 'vacation' I can stand."

They both laughed nervously.

"I guess maybe I'll do the same thing," Garth admitted.

They looked at each other, and Hilary wasn't sure if she had the strength to leave.

"I'll get the check," she said softly. "I have the money this time."

Later they rode to the Merrymont and quietly filled out the small mountain of insurance forms, then called the airport and made their reservations for the next morning's flight.

As they left the counter Garth put his arm around her and drew her close to his side. "Stay with me tonight."

"I was thinking about getting a room in town," she confessed. She knew that if she spent the night with him, she'd be helpless to leave when morning came.

"Please . . . one more night," Garth urged.

Hilary shook her head ruefully. "What am I going to do with you?"

Garth's adoring eyes sent her the silent answer.

"Oh, I almost forgot." She rummaged

208

through her purse after they were seated in the taxi. "Your money."

"Keep it. Consider it a get-acquainted present." Garth smiled.

"Thank you, but I couldn't." Hilary tucked the wad of bills into his jacket pocket.

Garth removed the money and pressed it firmly into her hand. "If you insist on paying me back, wait until you get home. Please."

"Okay, but I will pay you back," she insisted, realizing she didn't want to spend their last few precious hours together arguing. "I'll put a check in the mail tomorrow."

She suddenly sneezed.

"You getting sick?"

"I think I'm getting your cold."

"Hm!" He grinned and winked. "I wonder why!"

They shared their last few hours together in the beach house beneath a darkened sky now ablaze with glittering stars.

"It feels like I'm saying good-bye to my best friend," Garth confessed as he cupped her face and tried to memorize every feature in the soft rays cast by the lamp at the bedside.

"I'd like to be your best friend," Hilary whispered.

Garth sipped at her lips as if they were warm wine. "Granted, my fair lady . . ."

It was a long time before their passion could be appeased. It was late when they finally dropped into an uneasy sleep, still entwined in each other's arms.

During the night they slept fitfully, waking every hour to look at the hands on the clock.

When daybreak arrived, few words were exchanged as they rose and dressed for their early-morning flight. They carefully avoided looking at each other as they packed in strained silence.

At the municipal airport on the outskirts of West Creek, they sat in strained silence as they awaited the plane.

The short flight was uneventful, and all two quickly they had landed at Raleigh-Durham.

This time a lengthy delay, such as the one they had experienced three days earlier, would have been welcome, but both departures were running right on time.

Hilary's plane was the first scheduled to leave.

"Well, I guess this is it." She forced her voice to remain cheerful, although her insides were tied in knots.

"Yes, I guess it is." Garth ran a hand uneasily through his hair. "You will keep in touch?"

"Sure." Hilary smiled and patted the side of her purse. "I've got your number written in three different places." She knew she didn't need the reminders. She'd memorized the number before the ink had dried.

"Well, they're playing my song," she said as the second call for Flight 527 come over the intercom.

Garth suddenly reached out and caught her to him. "Take care of yourself . . ."

"You too . . ." She was suddenly crushed against his broad chest.

Even through the thick fabric of his jacket she could detect the beat of his heart. It was all she could do to refrain from crying out her pent-up love as he lifted her off her feet and kissed her more passionately than ever before. She was breathless and teary-eyed when the final boarding call sounded.

He gently lowered her back to her feet, and his eyes met hers solemnly. "I'm holding you to your word, Hilary. Don't forget me."

"I won't," she promised, and they kissed one last time before she broke away and ran blindly down the jetway.

Chapter Eleven

THE FOLLOWING DAYS PASSED with painful slowness. Hilary spent long hours at O'Connor Construction Company, where she was preoccupied with agonizing memories of Garth.

They both had remained true to their promise to keep in touch. They corresponded via telephone or cards almost daily.

Even Lenny Ricetrum had kept his promise to wash his hands of Hilary. He'd quit his job at O'Connor's, and someone had mentioned that Lenny was seeing a recently divorced brunette.

The news didn't bother Hilary. She discovered she didn't care if Lenny's newest flame had purple hair—as long as he stayed away from her.

The sound of the five-o'clock whistle signaled Hilary that Day Number Ten had passed. Feeling disheartened, she put on her coat and headed to her empty apartment. Gary Franks had called earlier and asked her out for dinner, but Hilary confessed she would be terrible company.

It was becoming harder and harder to face the four walls that had become her self-imposed prison. She fantasized that Garth would magically be there waiting for her one night, but she knew that wasn't likely to happen.

Hilary arrived home and held her breath with anticipation as she checked the mailbox. When her trembling fingers retrieved the large manila envelope with Garth's return address scrawled across the corner, she felt her heart soar. A big fat letter was stuffed inside. Hilary unfolded its neatly written pages, and a pink check slipped to the floor. She frowned, scooping up the check she'd sent to him for the clothing he'd bought her.

Trying to read the letter and unlock the door at the same time proved to be impossible, so she paused in savoring every word just long enough to jiggle the door to her apartment open. Once inside, she didn't bother to remove her coat as she sank down on the sofa to finish the letter.

"Oh, Garth, I miss you," she whispered, wiping the back of her hand over eyes that were now filling with tears as she read his casual chitchat.

The telephone rang, forcing her to restrain her tears. She grabbed for a tissue and prayed the caller would be Garth.

"Hi, honey!" Simon Brookfield's voice came cheerfully over the wire.

Feeling her heart take a nosedive, Hilary sighed. "Oh, hi, Daddy."

"What's this 'oh, hi, Daddy' stuff? Are you all right?" Simon had noticed that something had been bothering his daughter ever since she'd returned from vacation.

"I'm sorry. It's been a long day." Hilary apologized for her obvious distraction. "How's Mama?"

"Fine. She wants to know if you'd like to come for dinner tonight. We haven't seen much of you since you got home."

"Dinner? Tonight?" What if Garth should call while she was away? No, she couldn't take the chance. It was foolish to sit and wait for his call, but then Hilary would be the first to admit Garth had that effect on her.

"Thanks, Daddy, but I'm really tired tonight. I thought I'd take a nice hot bath and go to bed early."

"Are you sure, honey? You've been spending a great deal of time tucked away in that apartment of yours lately. We miss you."

"I'll make it up to you, I promise. Maybe one night next week."

"Okay, hon. Anytime will be fine with your mother and me. Just give us a call."

"I will."

"How's the cold?"

"I think I'm finally getting over it."

"You're sure nothing's wrong?"

"Dad, I'm not a child," Hilary reminded him patiently.

"I know, I know. But just because you're grown doesn't mean we don't still worry about you. You just wait—"

"Until you have children of your own!" Hilary finished for him, then laughed softly. "Okay, I'll make sure they keep me up nights worrying, just the way I do the two of you."

"You won't have to go out of your way to do that," Simon chuckled. "It comes with the job."

"Good night, Dad."

"Good night, dear. Don't forget about dinner next week."

"I won't."

Hilary hadn't much more than placed the receiver back onto its cradle when the phone rang again.

"Hello." She was careful not to allow her expectations to soar again.

"Hi, babe!" The familiar baritone voice immediately turned her knees to pulp.

"Well, hi there!" Hilary deliberately kept her voice casual, although she had to sink onto the nearest chair. "I just got your letter . . . and my check. What's the big idea?"

"Don't panic. I can explain."

"Then start explaining. And it'd better be good. If not, this check goes back in the mail —first thing tomorrow morning," she warned.

"You'd actually be so crass as to send a present back?"

"Present? What's the occasion for such a generous present?"

"Your birthday?" he offered.

"Uh-uh. My birthday isn't until July. How quickly one forgets," Hilary teased.

"I didn't forget . . . You never told me," Garth said softly.

"You never asked."

"Okay, I'm asking you now. When's your birthday?"

"July twenty-eighth."

"So I'm a little early. Take the check and buy yourself something nice."

"Oh, Garth! I love you!" The words were out before Hilary realized what she'd said.

There was a significant pause. Then, "You what?"

Hilary realized that her impulsive declaration of love had completely stunned him, so she tried to patch up the confession by appearing to make it more of a blanket observation. "Of course I love you. How could I not love a man who helped me through three of the most miserable days of my life?"

"Oh . . . that kind of love."

Had she heard a distinct let-down in his voice, or had she only imagined it?

"Exactly when do you think it happened? Was it when you soiled my handkerchiefs, or when we hand-wrestled for the Samsonite?"

Garth tried to mask his disappointment with teasing.

"I think it was shortly after you called me Harry," Hilary decided.

For a moment there was another silence; then Garth said, "Well, I guess I'd better get myself in gear and get ready for work. I just thought I'd call and see what you were up to."

"Garth . . ." Hilary stalled, wanting to tell him she did love him—and not just because he had shared those three days with her. She loved him because he was special. She loved him because he was Garth.

"Yes?"

"I'm glad you called."

Hilary was positive she detected a slight unevenness in his voice this time. "I think about you a lot, Hilary."

"I think about you too."

"Lenny giving you any trouble?"

"No, I haven't seen Lenny lately."

"Well, I need to go. We've been in school recently. They've started a new landing program that's designed to clear up the lengthy delays in flight schedules." Hilary heard his weary sigh. "It's been a nightmare."

"Is the weather bad?" She wanted to prolong the conversation, yet she knew she shouldn't delay him.

"It snowed a little today."

"Well, thanks for my birthday present."

"Yeah, keep in touch."

"Yes . . . you too."

"Good night."

"Good night."

The following week more presents arrived. First, Hilary received three dozen white roses. Garth called that evening to explain that their arrival was an early Valentine's Day gift.

Hilary accepted that. Valentine's Day was only three weeks away, she rationalized, wondering if he really thought the flowers would last until then.

When a large flacon of Joy was delivered two days later, it was Hilary who called Garth. Her jubilant thank you was casually dismissed with the assurance that the perfume was an early Christmas present.

"Garth, it's only the last day of January!" Hilary protested.

"Yeah, I know. But I like to get my shopping done early. I beat the rush of last-minute shoppers that way."

As the days turned into a full month, Hilary

knew their phone bills would be astronomical. She dreaded the day when AT&T tallied up their conversations.

The weather in Denver took a turn for the worse, dumping a record-breaking snowfall the first week in February. More diligently than she watched *Dallas* or *Falcon Crest,* Hilary found herself watching the weather report every night to see what the weather was doing in Chicago.

Until she'd met Garth, she'd never cared about the forecast. But with the increased pressures bad weather brought to the air-traffic controllers, Hilary's nightly prayers now ended with a Please, let there be clear skies in Chicago tomorrow!

Garth came to dread the long nights. After having spent two nights in Hilary's arms, he had yet to experience the restful sleep he'd shared with her in West Creek.

Scanning the forecast printout sheets for the Denver area, he wondered if his "snow bunny" would ever again melt in his arms the way she had at the beach house.

Sometimes Garth would call Denver on his break when he could feel the pressures mounting. Hilary could always tell when he was calling from the control tower. His voice would be tense. But after five minutes of chatting he seemed to relax and become his old self again.

"You're good for me," Garth confessed one night, and Hilary assured him that the feeling was mutual. She always felt warm and needed after they hung up, even in the loneliness of her apartment.

March arrived, and with it came Hilary's first phone bill. She let it sit on the coffee table for two days before she had enough courage to open it.

"Good grief!"

She knew she couldn't afford to keep up with the tremendous cost of calling Illinois every other night. It would be cheaper to fly there and talk to Garth in person.

She paused as she seriously toyed with the idea. Well, why not? For much less than one month's telephone bill, she could fly to Chicago and spend an entire weekend with him. She threw the bill in the air exuberantly. Why not?

It wasn't the huge phone bill that convinced Garth it was time to put a stop to the cat-and-mouse game.

He'd always come home tired, even before Hilary came into his life. But now he'd always wake up feeling exhausted, having spent night after night tossing and turning.

Garth didn't mind obsessing about Hilary during his every waking moment . . . he just preferred that she be in his arms while he was doing it.

He tried dating Lisa a few times but finally admitted that she was out of the picture. Lisa had taken the breakup as he'd expected—very badly. She was furious and nasty.

But Garth didn't care. All he could think of was Hilary.

Hilary, in the meantime, frequently drove out to Stapleton International Airport, where she would gaze longingly at the control tower. She tried to visualize Garth's world.

She was still debating whether or not to fly to Chicago. Suppose Garth would resent her for just dropping by. It was possible. He'd never once suggested they try to see each other again. In the end, Hilary decided that was a chance she'd simply have to take. She couldn't endure another week without seeing him. As she gazed at the distant tower, she thought of the man she loved who was hundreds and hundreds of miles away. The constant roar of jets taking off and landing reminded her of the awesome responsibility of

Garth's job, and she felt the sting of tears filling her eyes.

Garth needed her. He needed someone to come home to . . . someone who could share his life, someone who would love him . . . care for him . . . nurture him . . .

Garth Redmond needed her.

On her lunch hour the following Friday, Hilary purchased a late-night flight to Chicago.

It was the day before Valentine's Day. She would plead that she couldn't find a stamp and wanted to deliver his card personally. Garth could hardly object, since he had used much flimsier excuses himself when her presents had been delivered.

The afternoon seemed to drag by without end. Hilary spent most of the time correcting one typo after another on the countless stacks of invoices she'd attempted to type.

Ten minutes before the five-o'clock whistle blew, Hilary was out warming the engine of her car. She figured there was no sense in wasting precious time. This way, the motor would be purring like a kitten when she punched the time clock.

At exactly one minute after five she was out

the office door. She was home by five-thirty, a new record for a drive that usually took close to an hour.

She packed a sufficient amount of clothing and personal items to get her through the weekend, then took a taxi to the airport.

The night before Valentine's Day! Hilary's heart raced wildly with the knowledge that, with any luck, she would be spending it in Garth's arms. She prayed he wouldn't have other plans for the weekend. The thought was too disturbing to dwell upon.

Hilary exited the cab and raced toward the busy terminal, paying no heed to the small patches of ice still lingering on the walkways. All of a sudden she found herself slip-sliding across the frozen glaze, groping wildly to retain her balance.

Dropping the suitcase, Hilary grabbed for a handrail just moments before she would have spilled to the ground. But not quickly enough to prevent her left ankle from twisting painfully.

She grabbed the injured ankle and groaned out loud. There was something about Stapleton and her ankles that just didn't mix! She thought of the last "fly the friendly skies" effort she'd attempted and prayed this wouldn't be another disaster.

She took small comfort in the fact that the right ankle had since healed. It was her left one that was killing her now. Retrieving her suitcase, she hobbled on, praying that she wasn't on another roll of bad luck.

In a rush to board her flight, she limped right past the handsome man who was just dashing out another door.

Garth stopped abruptly and whirled around as he saw Hilary limping in the opposite direction.

He saw that she was carrying a suitcase, and his heart nearly stopped. She was on her way out of town just as he was coming in. The realization shot a surge of panic through Garth, and he called out to her hastily retreating form the first thing that came into his mind.

"Hey, what's wrong with your ankle?" he shouted, puzzled that, after all this time, she was still hobbling.

The sound of Garth's voice brought Hilary to a skidding halt. He *had* come for her! She knew it even before she turned around.

"Garth!" Hilary's eyes lit up like two Christmas trees as she dropped the suitcase and came flying toward him, forgetting all about her throbbing ankle.

Garth caught her up in his arms, and they kissed long and hungrily, ignoring the way they were blocking the flow of traffic.

"Garth, darling! What in the world are you doing here?" Hilary exclaimed as their mouths finally parted long enough to exchange a few brief words between snatches of eager kisses.

"I could ask you the same thing." Garth grinned. She looked even better than he had remembered.

"I . . . I was on my . . . I asked you first!"

"I'm here to see my girl," Garth said simply, then took her mouth in another possessive kiss.

It was forever before they could will their mouths apart long enough to step aside finally and let the other passengers pass.

"No kidding—why are you here?" Hilary insisted as he carried their bags over to the side and set them down.

"I was just passing through Denver, and I thought I'd stop in and ask you to . . ."

"I would love to have dinner with you." Hilary accepted before he could finish the invitation.

Garth grinned and kissed her once more. "Who said anything about dinner?"

"Oh, uh . . . I thought you were going to ask me . . . to have dinner with you," Hilary could feel an embarrassed flush spreading across her face.

"No. Dinner isn't exactly what I had in mind."

"I'm sorry . . . What were you going to suggest?"

"Well, since I couldn't find a stamp to mail your Valentine card I thought I would personally deliver it, and then—"

"Oh, Garth! That was my line!"

"Your line?"

"Yes! I was on my way to see *you*, and I was going to say I couldn't find a stamp for your card, so—"

Garth laughed and they were suddenly kissing again. When their lips parted much, much later, he gently cupped her chin and lifted her face to meet his. "I was on my way to ask you if you weren't busy this weekend, would you consider marrying me?" he finished.

"Marry you?"

"That's right."

"Well . . . yes. Of course."

"I was hoping you'd say that." Slowly his mouth covered hers.

All of a sudden his words sank in, and Hilary's eyes widened in disbelief. She broke off the kiss and let out a shriek of delight as she threw her arms around his neck and hugged him so tightly he found it hard to breath. "Marry you! I can't believe it! When? Now? Of course I will!"

Garth chuckled and tried to loosen her grasp but finally gave up and hugged her back. "Why do you find that so hard to believe?"

"You've never said you loved me," she said accusingly, still finding his proposal hard to believe. Garth had just asked her to marry him!

"Maybe I've never said it in so many words, but I thought you might get the hint," Garth chided. He thought of the horrendous stack of florist, phone, and department-store bills lying on his desk at home.

"Oh, I love you!" Hilary kissed him over and over, not caring in the least that they were making a scene. "To heck with all these flimsy excuses! Let's go to my apartment," she suggested in a breathy whisper against his

ear. "I want to give you your Valentine's gift
. . . in person."

Garth growled suggestively. "I hope it's
what I've been wanting for weeks."

Hilary winked. "I would have sent it earlier
if I could have found a big enough stamp."

Garth quickly picked up both pieces of luggage, and they started out of the airport, with
Hilary clinging possessively to his arm.

"Is your ankle still bothering you?" he
asked.

"Would you believe I slipped on the ice and
sprained it again?" she complained.

"Same one?"

"No, the other one this time."

Garth threw his head back and laughed,
feeling like a million dollars as they walked
out of the terminal into the frigid night air.

Snow was beginning to fall in thick, puffy
flakes that stuck to the frozen ground the moment they landed.

"The weatherman's calling for eight inches
by morning," Hilary warned.

"Well, naturally!" Garth looked at her
wryly. "What else would Brookfield and Redmond expect when they're together?"

Hilary grinned and wrinkled her nose at

him. "Say what you want, but I think we'll make a perfect team."

Garth leaned over and tenderly kissed away the remains of the large snowflake that had just landed on her cheek. "You bet we will, Brookfield. The *very* best."

Special Offer
Buy a Dell Book
For only 50¢.

Now you can have Dell's Home Library Catalog filled with hundreds of titles. Plus, take advantage of our unique and exciting bonus book offer which gives you the opportunity to purchase a Dell book for *only 50¢.* Here's how!

Just order any five books from the catalog at the regular price. Then choose any other single book listed (up to $5.95 value) for just 50¢. Use the coupon below to send for Dell's Home Library Catalog today!

DELL HOME LIBRARY CATALOG
P.O. Box 1045, South Holland, IL. 60473

Ms./Mrs./Mr. _____

Address _____

City/State_____ Zip _____

DFCA -5/89